SAVIANO SECRETS: A Mafia Murder Mystery

Christine E. Posemato

Copyright © 2022 Christine E. Posemato

All rights reserved. No part of this book may be reproduced, stored in a retrieval system, or transmitted, in any form or by any means (electronic, mechanical, photocopying, recording, or otherwise), without prior written permission from the publisher, except in the case of brief quotations in articles or reviews.

Cover design by Vila Design

Published by Van Rye Publishing, LLC
Ann Arbor, MI
www.vanryepublishing.com

ISBN: 979-8-9851099-2-4 (paperback)
ISBN: 979-8-9851099-3-1 (ebook)
Library of Congress Control Number: 2021949689

Dedication

For J, Dessa, Matt, Kay, and everybody else who believed in me. Love you!

In memorial of Jan Gray.

Contents

Chapter 1

The Present

The man kneeled behind cardboard boxes in an alley. The shadowy figure was visibly trembling, either from chill or panic. In truth, he didn't know. He drew his gray sport coat tighter around his chest as he kept control of the pistol in his other hand. The moon shone directly above him, casting a strange light through the alley. He feared that the secret he wished to carry to the grave would be discovered. It would happen before the evening was over.

He heard deliberate footsteps approaching him. The man gulped and cursed. Despite his best efforts to keep the other man from learning his position until he was ready, he was ill-prepared.

The new arrival yelled, "Jack Saviano, I know you're here! Come out with your hands above your head! I don't want to kill you!" Daniel kept his expression calm as he yelled, but he shuddered involuntarily, knowing he had to keep the shudder to himself to avoid alerting his quarry to his nervousness.

Jack, shocked by the other man's bravery, retorted, "There's no other choice." He hesitated. "I do not plan on being captured." A whimper escaped his lips. "I taught you to honor your elders." Jack frowned, concluding, "You should know better than to call me by my first name."

The younger man gritted his teeth. A long time had passed since he had seen his father. The estrangement had not been the son's decision. As memories invaded his mind, he urged himself to focus on the present. As he grabbed the gun from the holster under his coat, Daniel rested his hand on the trigger. He responded angrily to his father, "You didn't train me to do anything. I had to learn everything on my own." His tone was one of deep resentment. Though he was tempted to scratch his mustache, he resisted. When Daniel showed worry, his mustache always trembled. Parent and son shared the same pattern, as well as their black, wavy hair. Though, as Jack matured, his hair became wispy and silver.

The scowl on Jack's face was accompanied by a sinister grin. He chided, "You didn't seem to be paying attention to my lessons, my boy." He slid his palm along his slacks to remove a speck of what he thought was lint. It was a tiny snowflake. Only that one flake fell on Jack. "Daniel," he sighed, his Italian accent thick in his tone, "it's done. Please let me die. I am tired."

Jack's attitude suggested it wasn't literal fatigue but a metaphorical one. Nevertheless, he remained silent. If he protested, Daniel might hesitate in the judgment he would make over the next few minutes.

Daniel was surprised by the tender words. He considered withdrawing his hand from the gun. But a few seconds later, Daniel grasped the weapon in his hand and turned toward the boxes separating father and son. "No!" he shrieked. In that instant, his father rose, directed the pistol, and tried to shoot it. The slug ricocheted off the stone in the wall to Daniel's left, destroying it. The explosion deafened Daniel, but he ignored the sound and focused on the task at hand.

Having many hours of mandatory firearm training, Daniel discharged his firearm. His father's heart was seemingly pierced by the slug. In the next moments, Daniel's dad's eyes widened with awe and horrified recognition as he stared at the scene. In agony, Jack clutched at his heart, thinking it would prevent organs from oozing onto his white turtleneck. Then, he sputtered, and he jerked his head back, hitting the wall with a dreadful crack.

Jackson Charles Saviano seemed about to take his last breath. Shocked, Daniel slipped in the blood-saturated snow. He lost control of his firearm. But if the gun fired, it didn't matter to him. Daniel stopped inches from his dad's body after making the rest of the way there through the blizzard on his palms and knees. Despite knowing his father was dead, Daniel reached to touch Jack's wrist and check for a pulse. When Daniel found nothing, he collapsed to the ground. His heart pounded. For a moment, he stared up at the sky, his heartbeat echoing loudly in his ears. "Forgive me," he moaned.

After what seemed like an eternity, Daniel felt a slight pressure on his shoulder. He forced himself to gaze up into the eyes of the visitor, who was struggling not to scowl at his dad's body. "Hi," Daniel responded, clinging to the woman's palm with his free hand in alarm as she helped him to a stand. Dan removed his other palm from Jack and quickly replaced it with his handkerchief on the wound in his dad's heart, blocking the blood from dripping. Blood soaked Daniel's hand and the cloth.

The woman released her grip and gazed first at Daniel, then at the body. She'd seen enough corpses in her long career, and she realized there was nothing either of them could do to save the man. "Don't you think we should deal with it?" she proposed, frowning. Leah Matthews was never one to tiptoe around concepts.

It was absurd to Daniel to hear anyone refer to his dad as an "it," though, knowing his father was deceased, the term "it" felt right. "Leah?" Daniel arched his eyebrow in amazement. He realized she should not be there because of who she was—Jack Saviano's consigliere or second-in-command. "What are *you* doing here?" he asked. It shocked him he could even speak. He stumbled upon her name earlier that month after receiving a summary of intelligence on the Saviano family. He hadn't known until he came upon her notes inside who she *really* was.

Leah had posed as Jack's co-worker and a household friend for forty years. She grinned, adding to the younger man's confusion. She thrust her fingers through her wavy gray hair and slid them into her wool jacket pockets. "What difference does it make?" she asked. As she spoke to Daniel, her brown eyes never turned away from Jack. It

4

wasn't an unusual question to suggest in her mind, but in Daniel's, the thought sent his brain reeling.

A glimmer of recognition passed over Daniel's face. "Who *are* you, really?" he inquired as a memory started to take shape. He had pored over the details in the intelligence report, which simply identified Leah as Jack's second-in-command, but she had always randomly popped up throughout Daniel's childhood. It was as if she stayed in the shadows, somewhat unseen as events played out. She never directly interfered until now. He wondered why. *What's changed?*

Leah snorted and nodded toward the body. "I am who I am, Danny Boy," she murmured in response. The quick glance she sent him spoke volumes. He knew better than to push her for the information. "We have to move this bastard from the alleyway. Let me take care of that. You need to go someplace warm." She cast a glimpse into the sky. The snow continued to fall. Half a foot in all fell in the period since Daniel executed his dad. Leah glanced at her wristwatch. "Meet me at the diner across the street in a half hour." She moved closer to the body of the man she had worked with—or rather, against—since they met. Leah refused to look at Daniel a moment longer. Instead, she turned her attention to the task before her.

"Shouldn't we stick around for your backup to turn up?" Daniel frowned. "It's now a crime scene." He watched Leah as she slipped on a pair of black leather gloves. Daniel studied her, wondering if he should suggest helping. After a closer analysis of his blood-spattered

5

clothing, he thought better of it. He needed to go home and switch into clean clothes. They had already contaminated the crime scene.

Leah glanced at him, stopping what she was doing. If Daniel were conscious of what was taking place, he would have noticed that she slid a handgun into her coat pocket. It was *her* pistol. *She* shot Jack Saviano. But Leah was damned if she'd tell Daniel. She came for business. Leah knew the methods to evade everything going to hell. "No need to wait for backup. I have a cleaning squad. It's better that you don't know who they are. This *never took place*," she threatened.

Daniel nodded. He had trusted Leah over the years with many secrets. She never quizzed him, and he'd learned never to confront her.

Leah resisted the inclination to spit in the corpse's face. God, she hated Jack for wrecking her life . . . and Daniel's life. When she spoke, her words came out sharper than she expected. "Go! Do as I ask, boy," she demanded, scowling. "I'll dispose of this piece of crap. As for this being a crime scene, let's see what develops." Leah nodded and hoisted the lifeless body across the alley in a garbage bin's direction. She paused as she heard Daniel express a wail of despair.

Daniel nodded, accepted Leah's words, and strode away but hesitated at the alley entrance. "Leah?" he called. "Did *you* execute my dad?" The words flew out of his mouth before he could take them back. He winced when he saw the older woman's face twist up.

Leah scowled and snapped, "So what are you going to do if I did, boy?" Once more, she nodded toward his car, parked at the far side of the alleyway. "Get the hell out before someone spots us together or before I kill you as well."

Something in Leah's words made Daniel follow her gaze, and he nodded in compliance. He turned down the alley. As though his feet were caught in quicksand, he slowly walked toward the alley entrance but peered back at Leah. She waited there, considering the body at her feet in front of the garbage bin.

For a brief instant, Daniel thought his father exhaled but concluded he imagined it. He had studied enough corpses to know that sometimes they moved when the oxygen left at death was driven out from the body. But he had confirmed his dad's lack of a pulse. Daniel brought the collar of his coat up around his neck and shuddered. *Dad is gone*, he decided as he unlocked his car's front door and got in. The image played through his mind during the trip to his apartment. One idea in particular echoed in his mind, taunting him: *If Jack wished to perish, why did he look puzzled as he did?*

Chapter 2

The Past

Jack Saviano laid his feet on the rectangular redwood desk while he stretched out in the supple leather armchair behind it. It had been a satisfactory position for years. Jack sat forward, peeking at the Manila file on the counter, then opened it. Time to go to work. This was something he expected since receiving it four hours earlier. Jack shuffled through the documents. Someone was recording his "profitable" business activities. The statement in front of him confirmed the evidence.

"Leah?" he bellowed, positive that the woman stood behind the entrance. "Get your ass in here!" Jack passed a palm through his hair, and his eyes flashed with rage. A minute later, the door opened, and she entered. "Sit," he growled, nodding at the vacant leather armchair.

Leah glanced around but locked eyes with Jack as she noted the harshness of his tone. After shutting the door but not locking it, she crossed the office, sat in the vacant chair, and crossed her legs. "What is it, Jack?" she inquired. Leah had already viewed the reports and learned what they showed, but she feigned naivety.

Jack grimaced and rubbed at his mustache. He jerked the file closed before tossing it over the counter toward Leah. "Read these values and see if you can explain them because I've studied them for quite a while now, and I sure as hell can't!"

Leah reached into her coat pocket, drew out her eyeglasses, and slipped them on. She grabbed the register and opened it, thumbing through the documents. Sitting back, she gave a sharp whistle. "StanCorp is gaining strength and has done so for the previous four months," she mumbled. Closing the file, Leah raised her head, squinting at Jack. "I wonder why no one caught this," she murmured, removing her glasses and dropping them back into the same pocket. StanCorp was producing more profit than the other companies Jack invested in. The companies had all dropped the last five years of their existence, yet Stan-Corp rose substantially during the preceding weeks.

Jack replied in affirmation. "I was on the phone with Billy earlier." He glowered. Billy Wilson was Jack's Certified Personal Assistant and long-standing associate. "He confirmed it. He hedged when I investigated for an answer—tried to play me for a foolish man and denied he noticed something." Jack laughed. "That mess is being dealt with." He winked and leaned back in the armchair again, assuming his former position and clasping his palms in front of him. After a second of silence, he bellowed, swiping his fist across the counter, scattering papers. "No one, Leah, and I mean no one makes an ignorant man of Jackson Saviano and lives to tell about it!" The fire burned in his olive eyes, and he took a reflective sigh.

"Jack, I know," Leah responded, struggling to concentrate on him. The woman was imperceptibly shaking but kept her voice bitter. She would not let Jack beat her, not when she was this close to his ruin.

It was a foolish mistake letting Jack have the notes. No one was perfect, though—even a woman who had devoted most of her teenage years to being a house cleaner to finance her college tuition, then went on to work as an undercover operative for the FBI, serving under J. Edgar Hoover until he died in 1972. Leah rose and moved to the exit. As she placed her palm on the latch, she paused and shifted, confronting her boss. "Jack?" she inquired, her eyes falling once again on the paper.

He grunted at her. "Someone will take charge of the issue, Leah. I assure you! Now, if you'll pardon me, I have major work to sort out." Jack held his gaze lowered to the notes as he shuffled in the file, avoiding the woman.

Leah took the hint and left. When she got the chance, she'd make some phone calls.

Chapter 3

The Present

Daniel sat in the booth and spread his palms on the counter. He ordered a medium Pepsi and added enough ice to keep the liquid naturally sweet but not enough to stop the taste. Leah had not turned up. It alarmed him to think about what the woman might have done with his dad's body, but he was hesitant to inquire about it. It was a rule he long ago adopted, "don't ask, don't tell." It was the philosophy that served him for many years. He would continue with this rational policy for life.

Dan's belly rumbled, and he recalled he skipped breakfast and ate a hasty lunch. He knew not to eat. His stomach could not hold food, considering the recent developments. Daniel squinted at his wristwatch, contemplating how long Leah would drag out the inevitable. There were critical questions for her, and he did not expect to pussyfoot around the conversation he needed to have with her. The door to the diner opened, and Leah wandered in, saw him sitting in the corner, and strolled over to the dinner table.

Leah sat opposite Daniel and set her purse on the seat

next to her. She wiped her face with her palm. Leah was tense and battled to hold her emotions in check. She leaned back against the solid surface of the seat and stared into space. Her eyes did not fixate on Daniel or her surroundings. "Did you eat?" she inquired. It was a simple question to relax the atmosphere. His company had changed her clothes, Daniel realized, and was now wearing a deep-olive jogging suit.

"No," Daniel answered, glancing into his drink. The ice thawed. He groaned and took a sip, trying to keep from choking on the now-flat Pepsi. "I'm not in the mood to eat." He scanned the surrounding area. The restaurant adopted a twenty-four-hour-open policy, catering to the graveyard-shift employees. A few families sat on the opposite side of the restaurant. "May I buy you something?" he offered.

Leah laughed and waved her hand. "No, thanks. I ate a sandwich earlier." She was seeking to evade the obvious problem. She exhaled. "You wanted to find out which one of us shot your old man." It was time she revealed the story, or at least part of it. Leaning forward in the booth, her eyes locked with Daniel's. "Jack Saviano," she announced, "was slime. I executed him myself. I needed to stage it perfectly so you'd suspect you'd succeeded in doing it yourself." Her words were harsh and displayed an edge of bitterness. She paused and revealed nothing further, not meaning to rationalize why she shot Jack. Leah had promised someone she would keep the full story a mystery unless it was necessary to reveal.

12

Dan's eyes grew in dismay, and he struggled to breathe. Why set up the deception that *he* was the one who killed his father? He thought Leah cared for him and his dad, but she had lied about that. "Why do that?" he demanded of her. It was a reasonable question to ask.

"You will understand soon." Stretching her palms across the counter, Leah considered her next words. "I was working undercover for a high-level administrative agent in Jack's organization. If the truth got out and people learned I arranged that bastard Jack's death, my cover would be blown." Her eyes narrowed.

Daniel glared at her. "What job provides you the authority to execute someone in the name of justice and lets you frame an ally?" he demanded, declining to acknowledge what he speculated.

Leah closed her eyes, attempting to collect her emotions, and then she opened them. A slight grin crept across her mouth. She continued to stare into Daniel's eyes. "I work for the FBI," Leah declared, unexpectedly serious. "Someone inside the FBI ordered me to take out your old man." The grin widened, and Daniel shivered. There was more at play here than he had imagined.

Chapter 4

The Past

It snowed as Patricia Saviano entered their four-story mansion. She wondered why Jack insisted on building the home. She hated heights and berated him for it every chance she had. The hate started during her childhood days growing up on a dairy farm in Illinois. It was late summer. She and her older brother, Scott, were playing Hide and Seek in their parents' barn. They were in the hayloft, and it was his turn to hide. He hid behind the hay stacked near the intersection of the eaves. The hay bale slipped, and Scott fell to the loft floor. Patricia recalled the agonizing impact of his skull striking the floorboards. It still brought a shudder down her spine.

Patricia put the groceries away and retired to the den. They had a black-and-white television. She flipped it on and went back to the kitchen for a snack. After draining a Perrier bottle, Pat crumpled on the love seat, kicking off her black pumps. She rubbed one foot with the heel of the other. She yawned and stretched, having had a poor amount of sleep because the dreams had started again.

Patricia wondered when the dreams would stop. It had

been a long time since her brother's paralysis from the barn incident. Someone from the hospital took him away when their parents thought it was time. They never considered asking Patricia to take care of him. When Pat found out he passed away in a group home five months after that, it devastated her. Guilt weighed on her mind after Scott's accident and inescapable death from his injuries. She was the one who suggested they play in the barn.

She stared at the picture of Daniel beside the love seat and smirked. He reminded her of her brother. Her offspring was at his swim meet. Despite being in elementary school, he had been in the middle school division since he was mature enough to join. Dan had the most gold medals and decorations in the middle school's history. Pat expected him home in two hours. She placed his supper in the oven so it was there if he was hungry.

Patricia considered doing the same for Jack's supper. He would eat it straight from the pan if she let him. Jack was predisposed to have many idiosyncrasies. *He* worked for no one, but the rumors ran rampant: he had at least a hundred people working for *him*.

Patricia turned toward the television and then grimaced. A news program came on the screen. The reporter said something about the police having come upon a deceased body in a dumpster. The killer decapitated the victim, severing the skull from his body. *People*, Patricia thought, *are becoming worse by the second.* A description of the man was pending notification of next of kin. No further information was available. Patricia turned off the television as she noticed a pair of headlights in the window. Jack was home from the office, she realized. The doctor called earlier that day with vital information. She dreaded telling Jack.

After a minute, Patricia went to the front door to greet her spouse. When she did, he acknowledged her gaze with sheer fatigue. He left his briefcase by the armchair and squirmed out of his overcoat, his actions mechanical. He shuffled to the cabinet and grabbed a bottle of liquor, draining a glass. Jack said nothing but collapsed onto the love seat.

"Are you ready to eat?" Patricia suggested. She strode to the kitchen as she spoke and awaited her spouse's response before opening the oven to take out the roasted chicken she prepared for dinner.

Jack grinned, raising his eyes in his wife's direction. At first, he considered saying he had eaten before. But one casual smell of the chicken, and he was hooked. Patricia, by every right, was an outstanding cook. Her parents were professional chefs when they were not working the farm in Illinois. They trained her.

"Sure, darling," Jack responded and rose. He went into the kitchen and took two plates from the cabinet, arching his eyebrow at her. "Would you care to accompany me for supper?"

The words were soft, and her husband's behavior startled Patricia. She nodded and took out the chicken from the stove. "Daniel will be late tonight, so we should set aside a plate," Patricia explained, studying Jack through narrowed eyes. His manner surprised Pat.

"We'll save him a piece or two," Jack responded, winking at his partner. He helped her arrange the poultry on each of their plates and dished out the dressing she made. It was a homemade recipe that had evolved through the generations. Patricia used the traditional turkey stuffing technique but included a few drops of Tabasco sauce mixed in. No one could predict the "mystery" item. The mystery survived many dinner table conversations throughout the years.

Jack set their plates on the dinner table and set their place settings next to the plates. He stood by until Patricia was ready and drew her chair out from the table to sit. When she was ready, Jack moved the chair in for her. He sat on the other side of his spouse. The Saviano family members said grace before supper. Tonight, it was Daniel's turn, but he wasn't home. Jack picked up the lead and said a brief prayer. He wrapped his napkin around his collar.

Daniel joined his parents midway through dinner. The atmosphere was one of disbelief. Daniel did not understand why. The boy scarfed down his dinner, watching his parents through half-closed eyes. It was an exceptional meal. He told them as much.

The Saviano family's fate was altered by what happened next. Nothing could prepare them for the events that were on their way during the coming weeks. The exposure of Jack's secret life would create a panic never before experienced by Arizona. Two members of the family would lose their lives. For Jack Saviano and his kin, this was the end of the good life.

Chapter 5

The Present

After what seemed like an eternity, Daniel murmured, his tone exhausted, "It was eerie seeing my parents laughing and carrying on that night. I seldom saw the two of them so joyful." He gulped his drink, noting Leah's perplexed expression. "My mom was pregnant," he continued, grinning. "I found out later that night. My sister was born eight months later." He paused, getting out his billfold from his trousers pocket. His eyes were wet with tears as he opened the wallet and pulled out a small photograph. Daniel gave it to Leah. The young girl in the picture was not even ten years old. "Her name was Sara," he revealed.

Leah's eyes widened. Sara had lovely blue eyes, which pierced your soul. In the shot, the girl giggled at something off-camera and wore an elegant purple blouse and matching slacks. Her socks were silvery, and she wore black dress shoes. The young girl sat with her hands tucked in her lap on a bamboo chair. "Your sister was a stunning young girl, Daniel."

Daniel grinned and nodded. "Sara was exceptional, that's for sure," he admitted. "She had a handicap, though."

He took the picture back as he spoke, and Leah glanced at him. "The doctors diagnosed her with congenital hydrocephalus. They flat-out told our parents that Sara would be lucky if she lived past a year. A neurologist was available to oversee her progress. I believe she had a shunt placement not long after her birth. I was in elementary school and wasn't around much because I was active in every team sport. It was no good to my old man if I wasn't into athletics. Because he was into sports as a teen, I had to be, too. Later, I heard Sara was prone to epileptic convulsions, but I have not seen her in many years, not since I was young." He closed his eyes, trying to forget all those years that he had been ignoring Sara.

Leah's eyes widened, and she gaped, this time closer, at the picture. "Oh my God," Leah whispered, and she sank back in the booth. Leah said nothing else, but her head fell to her breast. "It's extraordinary. I never remembered her." She reflected to herself. In fact, she had noticed the girl but paid little to no attention to her back then.

"Dad valued privacy. We kept her confined to her bedroom until she was school age. For my dad, Sara's condition was an unprecedented problem. He cherished her, but he dreaded what she could and would do to his identity." Daniel took a breath, shrugging. Jack Saviano made sure Sara was entirely out of the community notice because he thought she would shatter his "ideal" family profile. Dan had never realized how much it disturbed his sister. Even now, many years afterward, it still puzzled him how inattentive he was to his sister.

"Do you mean his position as a prominent community leader?" Leah suggested, shaking her head. She growled the words out in hatred. For all Jack gave people in his life, he allowed his offspring to rot. This man pretended he cherished his family for his public benefit. No one ever figured out the people he loved least were his relatives. The woman clenched each of her narrow fingers over her hand to form a fury-driven fist to prove her utter disgust.

God, Leah detested Jack. Unlike her other assignments, killing Jack produced a plethora of desires within her. The prevailing of those being revenge. Her work did not usually present with such emotional entanglements, though. Each one was just a name on a note stapled within a mundane Manila file. Jack, however, was a rare exception. There was an intimacy with the depth of hatred that she bore for this man.

"You asked earlier why I pulled the trigger, Daniel." The words were icy. "I swore I would never admit my true motive to anyone concerning my career. But, Danny Boy," she smirked at the pet name, "you need to find out the truth after what you have shared with me about your sister."

"Wait. Before you tell me, I need to explain what I have learned about Sara. She lives someplace in Phoenix. Aunt Janice took her there. I found out two days ago. I assumed she was dead after what happened to her. I guess I thought she couldn't mentally handle what she experienced that night. The courts separated us and didn't tell me where she went. I was a kid, so I didn't have any say. But I found this on my desk recently. She is alive." He took out a file from under his coat and gave it to Leah.

Two weeks earlier, Daniel received a Manila envelope containing a picture of what Sara looked like now and her potential location. When he went home tonight, he would confirm the lead on Sara's likely whereabouts. He hadn't had time to look at the file completely. But he recalled learning that Sara commuted by a special needs transport van from Phoenix to Prescott for employment.

Leah frowned at Daniel. "Why did you think she was dead?" Leah had known the truth all along about Jack Saviano, Sara, and their family. But she assumed it wasn't her call to explain it to Daniel.

Daniel shrugged. "It was safer to accept that Sara died than face the guilt of what my monster father did to her if I thought she were still alive. He created every part of her misery." He hoped Leah would let it slip that she already knew about the circumstances concerning his sister.

Daniel recalled seeing the anguished look on his sibling's face when Aunt Janice came and took her away. He felt the panic that seeped from his sister's body as she clung to his hands in agony. *Leah knew, dammit. She knew.* It was eerie to him, thinking of the evening Sara left. She had clasped his hand so strongly that he had to extract her fingernails from his grip. The indentations were so deep, he believed he had permanent scars.

Sara's skills were so few, Daniel wondered if she would ever have a normal life. But it turned out Sara had developed a great deal from her childhood days to the present. She was an affluent attorney working with a prominent District Attorney in Prescott. Why Daniel had not kept track of his sister since the night she left was clear: he simply hadn't bothered figuring out whether she was alive. He never checked up on her. There had been so much blood that night that it made it easier for him to convince himself that no one survived. Since Daniel discovered his sister had kept a modest profile over the years, he assumed she was not happy being in the public eye.

Daniel felt an examination with the local Crime Scene Investigator of what had happened the night Sara left could defend his conjectures. His position as a lawman had gained him entry to the case files, which he and the investigator reviewed. Despite that, Daniel was still largely clueless about Sara's circumstances. For him, she died that night. It was safer if he did not press the matter. He doubted Sara thought *he* was alive either.

"Do you plan to see your aunt and clarify what happened, Daniel?" Leah demanded. She scrutinized him for a minute, awaiting a response. Janice had always admired her brother-in-law. In her eyes, Jack was the proverbial angel and unable to manipulate anyone, especially her sister, nephew, and niece.

Daniel lowered his head and inspected his hands. He clutched his cup so tight that his knuckles turned white from the pressure. "I have no clue. Remember, nobody back east knew dad was a convict. It would destroy her delusion of him."

Daniel drew a sharp breath and let it out. *No one knew.* The words reverberated in his mind until he swore he heard them spoken. Even Daniel himself didn't remember his dad's true personality. Daniel's thoughts drifted back to the file he had received about Sara's whereabouts. He turned to Leah and demanded to know, "Did you drop those files on my desk at the police station?"

The question was clearly an accusatory one, and Daniel's tone wasn't lost on Leah. She frowned and jerked, looking reminiscent of a deer caught in headlights. She nodded, dumbfounded. "Yes. Yes, I did. It was time you learned the truth." Leah studied him as she spoke.

Daniel frowned and considered his next words. Something was amiss. Sara is still alive. Was his *mom* as well? It terrified him to inquire, though he needed to know. "Leah," he started, a thousand memories reflected in his eyes as he whispered her name, "is my mother alive?"

Leah refused to look at him. Leah had been there that night, whether Daniel recalled it or not. She had to choose her words. Her eyes drifted over to the counter and searched the menu above the cash register. Leah refused to meet Daniel's piercing gaze. People had been coming in and leaving the restaurant for the preceding twenty minutes. People crowded the building.

"Preposterous," Leah responded. The lie was out in a second, and she cringed. "Your mother is dead," she insisted, tugging at her coat. Leah refused to meet Daniel's gaze, and tiny beads of sweat formed and trickled down her forehead. Leah promised to call Patricia later to alert her. Daniel still had no confirmation that she was alive.

Patricia had indeed lived, though. And Leah had brought her to a secret location and helped her change her identity. After Sara left with Janice, Patricia returned to her childhood home in Illinois. After surgery and the proper paper trail, she altered her identity for good. During that time, Pat lost track of her offspring. She inquired about Sara's whereabouts, but her daughter had seemingly vanished.

Daniel frowned. "I miss Sara, Leah," he blurted out. He spread his palms, still studying the African American woman seated across from him. "Tell me the truth. Quit lying," he pleaded with a grimace. "Where is she?" The epiphany that his mother *must* be alive came to him a minute after.

Leah gasped and blanched. She sputtered, her hands quivering. Her mouth became dry, her face fixed in bewilderment. She did not notice the skepticism on Daniel's face until she met his gaze. Daniel raised his eyes to Leah. But before glancing directly at her, he squinted past her and paled at what he saw. "Mom?!"

Daniel's mother, Patricia, smiled at the woman seated across from him. She relaxed on the seat opposite him as well, next to Leah. She set her handbag next to her and drew her palms across the counter. "Leah called me," she revealed. Patricia watched Daniel in silence, understanding his confusion. A flash of emotions played over his face: confusion, anguish, irritation, and turmoil were the major ones.

"Mom," Daniel murmured after an interminable silence, "I assumed you were dead. I saw the blood and your body. What the hell happened?" He was not sure who he focused the second remark to, Leah or his mom. He swore he'd get an answer, though.

His mother spoke. Her words were cool and deliberate. Somehow, Patricia had developed an accent. He didn't recall one from his childhood days. Dan wondered how it started. It was odd, but the accent sounded British. "Things aren't always what they appear. Leah, as you guessed, knew what occurred that night."

Dan resisted the inclination to retort, "Well, duh!" He squinted at the two women. Instead, he rose. "This will take time, won't it?" he inquired. Retrieving his wallet from his coat pocket, he asked, "Can I bring either of you something to eat or drink?"

Patricia nodded and replied, "I'll have a large Pepsi and a taco salad, no chives." She peered at Leah, who shrugged and repeated her earlier rejection of the offer. She was not hungry, she reiterated.

Daniel went away to arrange the request. Leah and Patricia exchanged wary glances. "It's a shame, don't you think, that Daniel will have to disappear now?" Patricia said. She cast a long glance at her offspring. "He realizes the truth now. I wish it didn't have to end this way. To execute my child wasn't part of the arrangement!" Leah nodded her agreement. "We have our crosses to bear,"

Patricia continued. "I admit, I loved watching you take care of that bastard husband of mine."

Daniel was moving back to the table as Patricia finished speaking. At the sight of her son, she had pangs of shame and guilt. It had to be this way. She came to accept it as a necessary course of action but wished it wasn't. Patricia knew what Jack Saviano did to Sara, and Daniel would eventually find out, too, unless she stopped it. She prayed Daniel wouldn't survive to find out. That was why she considered killing him. Patricia could not allow Daniel to discover the truth about what transpired the last night they were together.

Chapter 6

The Past

Jack had risen from the dining room table as his son entered the room. He studied his wife and then his offspring. "You're late," he declared.

Daniel detected a grimness to Jack's words but ignored it. He nodded, grunting. "I'm sorry, Pop. Practice went overtime." The answer seemed feeble, in the adolescent's point of view. He had, in fact, missed football practice, playing one-on-one basketball with some buddies instead. He hated football and preferred to play basketball. Jack was not a basketball star in school. He was a football champion and forced his boy to play the same sport. He did not care that Dan hated football.

Jack glowered at his offspring and signaled to his wife, clasping her hand with his own. He nodded twice, reiterating the action, inclining his head toward his companion. "I expected you to be here earlier than you were. Your mom and I have something important to say." Patricia stood behind her husband, her palm resting on his shoulder.

Daniel shoved his plate aside and gazed at his parents

in silence. He expected the inevitable shoe to drop, realizing something was wrong from how they continued glancing at him, to each other, and back to him. *Did they find out I ditched school last week? Is that what this was about?* He realized he had better stay silent until he was certain what it was.

Jack continued, with a mix of emotions in his tone. "Your mom is pregnant, son," he explained. There was no escaping the matter. Jack Saviano would never do something like that. He believed in a direct approach.

Daniel's mouth fell open, and his eyes widened in awe. "I'm going to be a brother?" he asked. "Do you have any idea whether baby will be a boy or a girl?" He refused to call the child an "it," even if they did not yet know the gender.

Jack and Patricia exchanged knowing glances and grinned at their boy. "Not yet. But we think it will be a girl," Jack explained, slapping Daniel on the shoulder with a smirk.

Chapter 7

The Present

Daniel laid back in the booth with tears wetting his face. He stared at his mom as though seeing her for the first time. In some ways, that felt to him like what was happening. He hadn't seen this woman once since the evening of the mass murder he assumed claimed both Patricia and his sister.

Snippets of memory entered his thoughts. He could see the pistol in his father's palm and hear his mom crying in bewilderment as the bullet hit her. Dan saw his sibling clutching at his shirt in anguish, her body rigid with terror. Daniel could not recall the quarrel that led to those events. But he now evoked the outcome with remarkable clarity. He recalled everything precisely as it had taken place, and he bit back a moan of indignation.

His mom was alive! How was that possible? She owed him an answer. That was the reason he gazed at her now, his expression savage. When he spoke, his manner was bitter. "What is going on? How are you even alive? How can Sara be alive? I see you sitting here tonight, but I don't know who you are! You owe me an answer, Mother!" He felt that if he chose that specific modification of her name, she'd realize how upset he was. The woman sitting at the table did not resemble his mother. Knowing this made it simpler for Daniel to pretend she was not the parent who supported him growing up.

Patricia braced her chin on her fingers and stared at her progeny. Several emotions played over her tired face, and the predominant one, torture, triumphed over the rest. Once she spoke, there were tears in her eyes. "Your old man was a bastard. That evening, after you went to bed, I confronted him with suspicions he had a liaison. We argued, with me blaming him and him denying all." She paused, choosing her words slowly as the recollections that overwhelmed her brain were grim. She was striving to keep a genuine expression. "You must have heard the argument because you came banging on our door. You recall, don't you, Daniel?"

Daniel nodded, remembering the argument now. But it was not the way she was describing it. Instead, *Jack* had accused *Patricia* of the affair. His mom was the one culpable for the indiscretion, Daniel recalled. He didn't understand why she was now attempting to deceive him. He needed to figure out her motive in doing so. Now was not the moment for allegations, though. When the time was right, he'd force the truth out of her.

Across from her son, Patricia tried to keep from shaking. Instinct told her that Daniel did not trust her account of who started the affair. *How*, she wondered, *could she satisfy him?* She knew if he did not trust her, she could not let him leave the restaurant alive. This man was her offspring and a man of the law. *Could she really kill him?* She had a headache but ignored the urge to rub her temples.

Daniel peered at his mom, and a thought invaded his mind: he wanted to confront her. "How did you know to come tonight?" He frowned again.

The woman squirmed in the booth. "Leah told me she would be here," Patricia whispered, closing her eyes. "She told me you assassinated your father and said she was going to tell you the truth about everything." Pat shrugged. Her face darkened. "Now that Jack is dead, he can't hurt anybody anymore."

Patricia sighed at the remark. Dead men couldn't hurt anyone. Yes, Patricia felt remorse for betraying her spouse. Yes, she regretted ever letting Daniel know she was alive. Patricia had many regrets. Her mind wandered to the month preceding the quarrel—to a time when Jack found her fit, rich, and eager and seduced her. Why he planned on killing her rather than divorcing her was not clear to her. None of that mattered now. She had vanished. And now Jack Saviano was dead. It was vengeance—justice was complete. Patricia considered her son for a minute, not talking. "What," she reflected, "could I say? I had to be here."

Daniel nodded once. The nod was deliberate. The many criminals he had arrested and interrogated during his career assumed his nod meant he acknowledged their claims. But he simply nodded to make them assume they had earned his confidence. It suggested he accepted them,

32

but he didn't. His senses told him they were covering up the truth. Most of the time, he was right. They didn't know Daniel was empathic. He felt emotions in people. That skill gave him the intelligence to discern when a suspect hid the truth from him. That was what his mom was doing. Daniel tried to prevent his anxiety and irritation from creeping into his words. "Is there another reason you stayed away so long?" He continued frowning.

His mother opened her mouth to reply. But she thought better of it and remained silent. Instinct told Patricia she should feign innocence. She knew she could not deceive Daniel anymore after all she had done over the preceding two decades. Patricia was tired of concealing the truth. She peered sideways at Leah and nodded. "I can't do it anymore," she said. She thrust her food aside and peered hard at her son. "Jack was a jackass. I loathed him. But not why you expect. *He* wasn't having an affair. *I* was." She snorted. Her expression became cynical from years of distaste for the man she had pretended to be Sara's parent. The truth was, Sara was *her* daughter but not Jack's. This fact she wouldn't tell Daniel directly, though.

Daniel took his cup of soda from the table. It surrendered its sweet taste now, but he didn't care. His throat was parched, so he took a sip to wet his lips. The liquid slid down his throat, and he choked on the taste. He crumpled in the booth, his back striking the plastic seat with a thump. He declined to talk. There was no satisfactory reason to talk. No words formed in his mind or on his

33

lips. The flat soda was bitter in his mouth and throat, but he forced it down.

"Who was the other man?" Daniel asked, recovering his voice. Daniel's hands shook with fury and horror.

"It doesn't matter," Patricia replied. "Just know that Jack did love you and Sara." She wavered for a heartbeat. "It was *me* he loathed." The pain made her utter her words with surprising intensity.

Daniel nodded and saw his mom had not touched her dinner. It was tepid. He lifted his eyes to hers, and, for the very first time, he recognized how evil and detached they looked to be. Oceans of darkness penetrated through to his soul, and he fought to keep from shaking. A thousand questions rushed through his thoughts. Daniel couldn't move his lips to suggest any, so he instead took a sharp breath. "I need a refill," he declared, as though that would end the issues he now endured. Dan needed to deny the images that wanted to go through his mind. He detested what he had done, or rather not done. He hated himself for not killing his father when he had the chance to on that night decades ago.

Deliberately, Dan shuffled to the soda machine, drained his drink, and refilled it with fresh ice and soda. Hesitating, he turned to study the women still seated at the table, concentrating his attention on the one he had known as his nanny. He now wondered who Leah really was, where she had come from, and why she had always seemed so relaxed around his dad, who made nobody else relaxed. As he noticed the exchange between Patricia and

Leah, it ignited the police detective's attention.

Something wasn't right, but he could not figure out what troubled him. Daniel sat back and set his drink on the counter. He peeked at his wristwatch. It was four in the morning. Four hours had passed since the nightmare had started with the incident in the alley. Daniel looked at Leah again.

As Daniel continued to stare, the odd sensation nagged at him. *What's wrong here?* he challenged himself. Instantly, he realized. "Gesu Cristo!" ("Jesus Christ!") He uttered the name of his Savior as a vulgarity. "La Croce!" ("The Cross!") He moaned in alarm. He returned to the table and confronted Leah. "You're wearing my dad's crucifix!" He raised a trembling finger toward Leah's breast, stopping at the silver- and gold-plated cross that hung around her collar.

Leah glanced at the cross around her collar. She hadn't been wearing it when she shot Jack Saviano. *He* had been wearing it. Why did it take Daniel so long to realize it was now around her collar? Why was it there? What relevance did the crucifix have for her? It did not belong to her. Jack had it. Like an apocalyptic dawning, Daniel realized. *Everything* made sense now. *Dammit!* "You weren't just Jack's employee . . . he was your son!" Daniel paled.

The two women glared at him in incredulity. Leah sighed, and her manner betrayed her body's response. "You better have evidence to back this up, Dan." She hissed. Her brown eyes flashed with impatience.

35

"The crucifix," Daniel reiterated, closing his eyes and remembering. The past echoed once again in his mind, and he clarified. "Dad informed me years before it was a present to him from his mom. He barely talked about her. He let it slip once that she was near but never revealed her identity to anyone. Shock registered on Daniel's face, and he asked, "Dad was *white*, wasn't he?"

Leah laughed, and a heavy burden removed from her shoulders. She stared at Patricia, who scowled and shrugged. Patricia thought to herself, *Tell him everything. It won't matter anymore. I will have to kill him once he's learned the truth anyway.*

Leah turned toward Daniel. "My son . . . Ah, yes. He was the child of a white father and a black mother. We fled away together, not that it matters now. Trying to raise him back in those days was problematic. We dealt with it as best as we could. He kept our identities secret. Even altered his name so no one learned the truth about who his parents were." Leah laughed. "Damn him for joining the mafia and making us gangsters!" She shook her head and felt the crucifix that hovered around her collar. "I removed this from your dad tonight, before I disposed of his wretched, traitorous corpse. Later, I slipped it on my neck and begged God that you would see it."

"So, who am I? If Saviano is not the family name, what is it?" It was a natural question, considering the recent discovery.

Leah and Patricia exchanged yet another glance with each other. Leah exhaled and gulped hard. "Jackson Allen

Cartwright was my child's proper name," she replied.

The name did not intimidate men. Daniel decided he would keep the last name Saviano because it succeeded even though, unlike his dad, he was not a mafioso. Instead, as a lawman, he enjoyed the power of making certain the scum of the earth (or at least of the city of Prescott) ended right where they belonged: behind bars.

Daniel took a sip of Pepsi and grinned at the two women seated before him. Looking at his wristwatch, he advised them, "It's getting near dawn." He tried to conceal a yawn.

The women responded in understanding and stood in a simultaneous motion. They moved to the other side, where Daniel sat gazing at his class ring on his index finger. He was having a hard time accepting that things ended up this way. Daniel rose and hugged the women. They felt hot against his cold frame, and he laughed, drawing in the smells of their soap and perfumes. They smelled of vanilla and lavender. He thought about this. Why did they smell the same? The answer came to him almost as soon as the query did: they had come from the same place. Daniel's grin faded, and he asked them, "Where are you staying?" The home Jack and Patricia had lived in was sold years ago. Daniel thought they wouldn't be there unless the new owners allowed them to lease a room. The prospect of that was a million to one.

Daniel had visited the home himself at one point, and the owners seemed unconcerned that he, a member of the Saviano family, had once lived there. But they felt irritation at knowing he wished to visit the dwelling. Dan thought they were right. He was violating their home and their right to privacy. Dan had no excuse for being there. Still, the prospect of standing in the place that began the end for the Saviano family was fascinating. It had kept him awake for the prior two weeks after Leah called to tell him that his dad demanded to have an appointment with him.

Daniel had tried to avoid meeting Jack, but Leah proved to be convincing. She told Daniel she was not expecting Jack would last much longer due to poor health. Leah said Jack asked her to locate his offspring. The old man claimed to want to resolve some of his offspring's skepticism about what transpired the night of the mass murder (what Daniel *thought* was a mass murder). That revelation made Daniel want to learn the full story. He conceded to face his dad. They had met in an espresso shop, eaten, and sought to avoid conflict. But there was an unpleasant quarrel. The manager threatened to toss them out and a chase ensued, ending in the alley.

The morning after Leah had called him, Daniel went to his office and discovered the Manila folder with his name handwritten across the center and a box full of files. Inside the files were many photographs and documents spanning half a century. There were original reports from the night his parents argued over the affair. And there was a report about Sara going to live with Janice, after which she and Daniel never saw each other again.

Daniel closed his eyes, squeezing them, producing

pain. He then jerked back to the present. He grimaced, realizing he was holding the two women in his arms, and he let them go. He nodded his head toward the exit. "You had better get going. It's been a hectic night."

Leah nodded, agreeing, and she shifted her hand in his, placing something in his fist. "Here's my business card, sweetheart." She winked, and he grinned. "I guarantee I won't let another twenty years pass without seeing you," she murmured. She kissed him on the cheek and glanced at her daughter-in-law.

Patricia told Daniel, "We're staying at the Colony Inn, Room 110." She knew she didn't have it in her to kill him after all. So, with those words, they left him alone. Daniel picked up his cup, emptied it, and saw the untouched meal as he returned to the table. He went to the cash register, asked for a sack to carry the food, and took what was handed to him.

Five minutes later, Daniel climbed his weary body into the driver's seat of his sedan. He did not see the black van parked near him as it pulled from its parking spot and trailed behind him.

Chapter 8

The Past

"**W**hat if he catches us?" There was a trace of panic in the speech. Patricia held a man, who was not Jack, in her arms. He had uttered the words. The guy was her husband's best friend and partner, Michael Gene Cromwell. Someone introduced Mike to Jack decades before, in high school, and Jack eventually gave his friend a position as a stockbroker in his criminal enterprise. Mike met Patricia at a cocktail reception the firm gave, commemorating the agents of the year. The allure was instant and reciprocal.

Patricia giggled, moving to clutch her lover's hand. "Quit worrying so much!" she countered, planting kisses all over Michael's neck. Patricia grazed a nail through his chest hair and grinned. "Sweetheart, you're so uptight. Jack is stupid, I assure you. He is so gullible, it's pitiful." She chortled and moved her hand over him. Patricia caressed a part of his anatomy he granted only one previous woman in his life to touch.

Michael writhed as Patricia drew her nails along his anatomy, tormenting him. He strove to regulate his breathing. Michael found it useless to talk. He exhaled and gasped for air. Her grip stiffened over him, and as she caressed him, she devoured his mouth with hers, silencing any noise he might produce.

Michael swallowed. He chewed his tongue and did everything in his capacity to try not to shriek. "It's not Jack I'm concerned about, darling." Mike leaned his head toward the door, and Patricia realized he referred to Daniel.

Patricia shrugged. "Do you think I'm foolish, Mike?" she spat while freeing him. Her eyes blazed and became disheartened as she clenched her hands into tense fists. "I wouldn't call you over here if I assumed someone would find out."

Michael shut his eyes, knowing he ruined the atmosphere. "I'm sorry," he mumbled, passing a palm through his blond hair. Mike placed it on Pat's heaving shoulder. He had made her weep. *Dammit.* He grumbled, "I better dress and go home."

Patricia gazed at him, lifted her chin, and nodded in understanding. "You're right," she said. She continued, "Jack will be out of the city the whole week if you want to come back. *Mi casa es su casa.*" As she spoke the proposition to Michael, Patricia sensed he wouldn't come back again—at least not as a lover. Michael slipped back into his brown suit, and Pat dipped her head in misery.

Patricia overheard a commotion at the bedroom door. It swung wide, and Daniel stood there, bathed in the powerful yellow glow of the hall light. He peered at his mother and the guy he did not recognize. Without speaking a word, he spun on his heel and returned the way he came. Patricia and Michael traded stunned glances and parted ways.

Chapter 9

The Present

Daniel awoke from the nightmare in cold perspiration, pushing out the vision of his mother's liaison. They had never spoken of her indiscretion, as though it never transpired. But two days after it happened, Jack confronted his spouse about the fling, which she denied. Daniel recalled his mom was then "executed" along with Sara, or so he had convinced himself. The images flooded back to him now, this time with amazing clarity.

Daniel sat up in bed and mopped his forehead with a trembling palm. He worked to breathe as the dreams disappeared from his mind. *Everything was a lie.* His dad wasn't the father he thought, and his mom may not have been the earnest, God-fearing woman he entrusted with his life.

Daniel tossed the blankets aside. He got up from the bed and worked his way toward the restroom without turning on the lights, although it was pitch black. Once in the bathroom, Dan locked the door and leaned against it. He let out a trembling sigh, which rattled in his chest. Daniel shut his eyes against the visions that were still demanding to burst through his thoughts. He staggered instinctively for the sink.

Regaining his logical thinking, Dan clicked on the light and studied his image in the mirror. He had taken a shower before meeting Leah at the diner. But his soul was more in need of cleansing than his body. There were no traces of blood on his clothes. Despite that, he was paranoid it was on the shirt he was wearing. He surveyed the gray material, relieved to know there was no crimson smudge on the fabric.

Daniel continued to stare at his image in the mirror. Terror gripped him like a rope around his collar when the figure looking back at him resembled his old man. *God, I'm going crazy*, he thought, blinking several times. After a few moments, the picture shifted to his actual mirror image. Daniel sighed and pivoted to the toilet. He made it before the meal he ate a half-hour earlier spilled into the basin. Daniel wiped his lip with a bundle of toilet paper and flushed the slime away.

Coming back to the master bedroom, Daniel glanced at the clock next to his bed and ran a palm through his hair. He realized it was five-thirty in the morning. He fell asleep for just an hour after he came back home. Daniel went to the living room, crumpled on the sofa, and leaned backward. He blew out an inaudible sigh and closed his eyes. Daniel wouldn't go back to sleep. For now, he was content relaxing. He braced his head against the many plush cushions he used while working, and he made himself as relaxed as he could. It would be an exhausting day tomorrow.

A half-hour later, Daniel knew he would not have a decent rest. He reached for his cell phone and called the police station. The desk clerk answered the phone. Daniel informed her he was ill from a virus and claimed he had to make an appointment with his physician. The lie was a conceivable one for him because Daniel felt nauseous and feverish. As if on cue, his belly twisted.

Dan made it to the toilet before clearing his stomach of the residues of his supper. Scowling, he undressed and climbed into the shower once again and washed off the smell that coated his body. He felt drained the second time. Returning to the bedroom, he put on his freshest pair of dirty slacks and a long-sleeved shirt. He'd wash his clothes later.

Padding with bare feet to the kitchen, he strode over to the cabinets, pulling out a packet of Alka-Seltzer. Grabbing a mug, he filled it with tap water and added two tablets. He watched for a few minutes for them to break down, and then he drained it. He hated drinking the substance, but it settled his stomach. The coffee in the kettle was still fresh. He poured a cup and brought it with him.

Daniel rarely drank coffee, just offered it to his visitors. This morning was an obvious exception. Dan hardly ever had time for guests anyway, an evidential fact from the residence's near-perfect cleanliness. He moved to the couch and sat, feeling the pressure of the world on his shoulders. Setting his mug of coffee on the counter, he gave a cursory search of the apartment for the TV remote.

Dan found it under a stack of week-old papers.

He pushed several buttons to turn on the set. Seeing the screen was still black, he muttered profanities that made a sailor blush. Daniel realized the batteries were dead. Flipping on the light by the lounge, he moved to his desk. He had bits and pieces in a drawer he long ago deemed his "junk drawer." Digging through it, he noticed the correct ones that powered the controller and dropped them in. Dan turned on the television.

Settling back on the recliner, Daniel expected to find the announcement of his father's assassination as a top story, but nothing of the sort appeared. It was simply a matter of time, though. Daniel knew this much and a few more details. He hoped no one knew that he had found out about his father's secret life as a mobster and about those who Jack Saviano destroyed to preserve his code. Those were unpleasant memories. Daniel wished he could ignore and even hide them. He was confident he could do both. But first, he needed to admit to himself that he was the offspring of a mobster.

The prospect made him ill again, although this time his stomach settled as he concentrated on the television screen. Nothing good was on TV at that hour, except the usual black-and-white films he grew up watching and a few reruns of various sitcoms. Daniel watched his favorite show from his younger days, "Quantum Leap," but he found his thoughts drifting again. This time it wasn't his childhood but two weeks ago when Leah Hartman, who he thought had died from a heart attack years earlier, called him from a remote area. It shocked him to hear her voice again. Had she not revealed who she was, he would have never known it.

"Dan, we need to talk," she announced. "I have knowledge of your dad's whereabouts. You need to see what I have." Leah hung up after agreeing to deliver the information.

When Dan came to work the next night, he saw the giant cardboard box comprising four decades of notes, documents, and reports. Various portions of intelligence were there, as well as separate files comprising the obits for his mom and Sara. The obituaries upset him and brought that awful night fresh into his mind. No matter how much he fought, he couldn't prevent the unpleasant memories from coming back.

Chapter 10

The Past

Jack scowled at the man sitting across from him, and his eyes were ice-cold with scorn. They were in Jack and Patricia's kitchen. Michael kept throwing Patricia a nervous glance, but she refused to face him. It was not because she did not want to but because if she glanced at him, Jack would lose his temper more than he ever had before.

Patricia recalled several times when Jack lost control. There were bruises on her shoulder from the last time he did. She refused to acknowledge Michael's silent pleas for help and instead focused her attention on dishing out two dishes of ice cream, one for her and one for Jack. Patricia's shoulders hunched over, and her mouth was set in a rigid, furious line.

Michael was the only one without dessert. Jack made certain of that. "You already ate yours, you son of a bitch," he growled, balling his palms into fists. Jack refused to call him by name. He was livid. Again, Jack's fingers stiffened in rage as his eyes flashed a furious crimson in the lamplight.

Michael did not know how his boss discovered he was screwing Patricia. Because Daniel walked in on them the night before last, Michael suspected the youth was to blame. Michael had declared that if he were to survive the impending hours, Dan would surely suffer for being the loose-lipped informant that he had turned out to be. The blond-haired young man swallowed the bile appearing in his throat. He trembled inside from the worry of death. He knew Jack always carried a firearm in his coat, even at home. "What do you propose to do, Jack?" The question had tormented him for years, considering the affair was going on for that long.

Michael was aware that the young woman in the next room was actually *his* child and not Jack's. But he was not sure Jack had realized that yet. Jack paused at the kitchen sink. His back was toward the window, with his palms resting in his trouser pockets. If he wished, he could have easy access to his pistol.

Jack took a breath and laughed. His face was neutral. "So," he drawled, exposing his milky-white teeth in a wide-mouthed grin, "what do we do now? Should I let the two of you carry on? Pretend I am oblivious my wife is screwing my strongest ally? Or should I end it? Ah, so many options!" Jack sneered and winked at Michael, who was squirming and sweating on his chair.

Michael was sure Patricia was clueless about her husband's "other career." But he was also sure she knew Jack had access to a gun. She saw him use it when Jack surprised a "burglar" at the home a week before. The fellow (who was really Michael) disappeared, much to Jack's annoyance. Jack had identified the intruder but knew he needed to stay silent because he did not want to frighten his family. He vowed to make the man pay for his treachery during their next encounter.

Jack grabbed Michael's arm and led him from the room. Nobody would ever see Michael again.

Chapter 11

The Present

Daniel wondered how he could so precisely recollect that particular memory from so many years ago despite not being able to recall much else going on around that time. He glanced at the table before him, and his mind fixated on the present. Although he needed sleep, Daniel knew if he went back to sleep, the nightmares would continue. That was something he did not want to happen.

Daniel rose, crossed toward the window to his left, and remained there for several minutes, wondering what he should do next. *Should he make breakfast? Should he try to work?* The pile of journals Leah had given him lay on the dining room table, beside his laptop computer.

Running a hand through his hair, Daniel powered on the laptop, opened a web browser, and searched for *Sara C. Saviano*. The search results came up with forty-six suggestions. To limit the search more, he entered the workable locations she may now be, including Arizona. Dan accessed various "people search" sites where he was a member. He limited the inquiry to the eventual two prospects: one in Phoenix and the alternative in Prescott

Valley.

Dan had brought up Prescott Valley on a hunch and cross-referenced his mother's name to confirm there was a match. The result came back positive, and Daniel's heart rose into his throat, his suspicions now supported. His mother and grandmother had told him the truth. Sara was still alive.

Daniel leaned back against the recliner and looked up at the ceiling. He ran a palm over his face and felt it was damp. He realized he was weeping. Dan wondered if it was from tears of joy, satisfaction, or regret. Considering he thought his sister was dead, like their mom, he supposed the tears were from joy. He glanced at the time on the microwave display and sighed.

Five-thirty in the morning. Sara was surely waking up by now, he guessed. Dan copied the home and work phone numbers and addresses he discovered and took a Styrofoam cup from the kitchen. He poured hot cocoa and made certain he was presentable.

Daniel didn't know what he'd do when he met his sister. He thought she would recognize him, though. He wouldn't need to say much except the routine hello. The rest of the dialogue was up to her. Grabbing his car keys and coat, Daniel walked toward the exit to find the sister he had not seen in two decades.

* * *

The building appeared as archaic as time. Dark red bricks had turned pale brown from two hundred years of sleet, snow, and other weather. Stenciled in gold lettering into the stone were the names "Atwater, Marcus, and Saviano, Attorneys at Law." Jason Atwater had founded the law firm with Miriam Marcus and Sara Saviano. When he passed away in a boating mishap, his successor David took over the company. Sara and David had been a couple. But the relationship ended when Sara admitted she was dating someone else. It hurt and shocked David when he discovered the individual was Miriam Marcus.

Daniel stood before the building, pushing back tears. He swallowed to contain himself and stepped through the sliding door leading into the lobby of the complex. The inside construction of the building was a post-Renaissance pattern. A receptionist studied a stack of reports in front of her. When Daniel approached, she discarded it. She folded her palms, and Daniel thought she was attempting to appear busy. She wore a deep purple pantsuit and a contemporary white turtleneck. "May I help you, sir?" the black-haired woman inquired, her eyes narrowing in skepticism. She asked, "Are you a cop?" Her smile was patronizing.

Daniel stepped backward, clearly shocked she had identified him as a police officer, considering he was wearing ordinary clothes. "Yes, I am," he confirmed. "But I am here to see Sara Saviano on a personal matter," he went on. Daniel leaned across the counter and noticed the lady drew a sharp breath, inhaling his cologne. "Is she busy?"

The woman grinned. Her eyes strayed to his pants

zipper. She gazed at him, blushing as if she realized what she had done. "You get right to the point, don't you? That's the trouble with cops; you're always so obvious." Her grin faded, and she leaned back, tapping her lips with her fingers. "No, Sara isn't busy," the woman admitted, obviously pleased. "She's right here." She straightened up, reached for a pair of crutches, and edged her way around the counter to stand in front of him.

Daniel took another step backward, and his eyes widened in astonishment. In a flash, he recognized the lady as his sister. "Sara," he murmured so quietly that he wasn't certain he said something, "I think . . . No, I . . ." Dan paused. He knew he was stammering, but he couldn't quit. He asked, "I thought you were a lawyer?"

"Sir," she rebutted, frowning, "you have me at a disadvantage." She narrowed her eyes and thought: *Who is this gentleman? He knows who I am, although I don't remember him. No, wait . . . His eyes. They seem so familiar. I'm positive I've seen him some place.* When Sara realized who he was, she huffed in a horrified exclamation. *No! No! Oh my God, no! It can't be, can it? Christ!*

Sara kept her thoughts to herself. "Actually, Sara stepped out to pick up breakfast. She'll be back in fifteen minutes. If you wish to wait . . ." She was trying to make it appear she didn't remember him. It was obvious she had failed, and she sighed helplessly.

A weak smile crossed Daniel's face as he realized Sara recognized him. "No, dear, I want to talk with *you*." He winked, continuing, "You *are* Sara Saviano, aren't you? You *are* my sister."

Sara nearly lost her equilibrium at his accusation. "Fuck." She snorted and searched the office, her eyes wide. "Bastard," she moaned under her breath, referring to him. "You win," Sara whispered. She sagged against the edge of the desk, weak from the pressure of having stood vertical. "Yes, it's me," she mumbled flatly.

Daniel's sister narrowed her eyes at him. "We can't talk out here. Sue Ellen won't be here for another . . ." she trailed off in mid-sentence and glanced at the clock on the wall behind Daniel, then continued, "two minutes." She giggled as she watched a woman come through the door, carrying several sacks of food tucked under her arms. "Then again, I have been mistaken before. There she is now."

Sara waited until the young woman had resumed her position behind the counter and handed her the bags. Then, Sara instructed her, "Sue Ellen, don't interrupt us under *any* circumstances. Before you remind me of the testimony at ten, please call and postpone it. I will get back with them in the morning." Sara arched her eyebrows at Daniel for approval, and her brother nodded. With that, Sara led him to her office, down the corridor.

Once inside, Daniel nodded in approval at his surroundings. Sara shut the door behind them. Diplomas and pictures of her and Miriam lined the walls, and a few more images were spread around her office. Sara moved over to her desk, slumping in the armchair. Daniel recalled she constantly battled for independence in the face of her disability. He respected her for that. "It's been a long time, Sara," he stated after a minute of the two studying each other in silence. He smirked and crossed his arms.

Sara nodded and gazed at her older brother in silence. She was watching him, and her eyes roamed up and down before she spoke. "Mom informed me you'd seen her and requested to locate me," she admitted, her tone harsh with concern. "The old cow didn't specify why, though. I expected better from her. She never could be sincere with me." Sara frowned at the picture of her mother in front of her. Daniel hadn't looked at this one in ages. The shot was from when they were kids. He recalled the moment as though it were yesterday. They had gone to the carnival. Sara and Patricia posed beside a mock ghost house.

Daniel grinned at the memory. He had taken the picture, and he remembered his dad refused to come that night. Turning back to Sara, Daniel spoke: "Did mom tell you why I organized the meeting with Dad last night?" He was straightforward because he sensed Sara was not one for small talk. The "meeting" had led to the confrontation between the two Saviano men. Jack had left the restaurant after the argument at dinner, and the chase began. Daniel was curious to know how much his sister knew. Their last night together was a distant memory— one he had buried deep in his subconscious until he received the dossier from Leah. Until yesterday, he assumed that his mother and sister had died.

Sara waved her hand dismissively. "No, she didn't

say," she countered, "and I didn't want to discover why, either." She ran her palms across the desk. "And Daniel, I don't give a damn why you contacted us after so long. You have not talked to us in twenty years. Why now?" Her shoulders dropped, and she glowered at him, waiting for an answer.

"Sara," he explained, "I am aware I've not been the greatest brother in the world. I could have stayed in the family business. Dad expected it of me, and Mom needed me to." He shrugged. "I didn't recognize what that business was, though, Short Stuff." He grinned at the nickname he gave her as a youth.

Sara stayed stone-faced. Her remarks were bitter when she talked. "The family business?!" she spat in indignation. Sara threw up her hands and growled, "Goddammit, Dan! Jack Saviano, our dad, tried to *slaughter* us! *That* was the freaking family business!" Sara's blue eyes flashed in fury. "He shot at me! And he shot at mom! The bastard left us for dead! Oh my God, you are a spineless coward for not remembering. You ran out of there like the chicken shit you are!" Hot tears streamed down her face, and she balled her hands into tense fists. Her frame was shaking in rage. Sara stopped mid-rant and took a shuddering breath.

Daniel said nothing, allowing his sister time to calm herself. When he finally spoke, the tone was calm, and it startled him how composed he was. "I swear, I didn't have any recollection of what he did that night. I vaguely recall a disagreement between him and mom, and the next minute there was blood everywhere. You were screaming. Mom was crying, covered in blood. I stood there, yes! I'm ashamed to admit I did. I didn't understand what was happening. I couldn't move, and I froze." He stuttered, struggling to remember more about what happened that night so long ago. Daniel needed to remember, if not for his peace of mind, for Sara's. "When I could make my feet cooperate, I heard dad shouting to get the hell out before he killed me, too. I ran and must have fallen in the uproar." Daniel swallowed the bile forming in his throat. He remembered falling onto the blood-soaked floor.

"You useless piece of shit! You didn't come back to see if mom was alive and didn't even consider checking for me!" Sara hissed through her teeth. The allegation was there, and Sara did not withhold the bitterness she felt. "God, I wished dad would catch your pathetic ass. I prayed he'd do to you what you allowed to happen to us!"

Daniel caught his breath, holding it for what seemed like an eternity at his sister's remarks. When he responded, his words were quiet. "He *did*, Short Stuff." He paused and continued, "We encountered each other last night."

Sara's knees bent, and she practically crumpled to the carpet beneath her. She straightened at the last second, and Daniel breathed a sigh of happiness. When he was sure she was safe, Daniel nodded. He gazed at the photo again, picked it up, and squinted at something in the corner. He hadn't spotted it before, and he blinked in amazement. Jack was standing in the back, out of the camera's focus. He had always been there, watching them throughout their lives, hadn't he?

"Yesterday morning, Sara, he came out of hiding. He wanted to kill me. No, that's not quite right. He wanted *me* to kill *him*." He nodded. Daniel was talking to himself more than to his sister. "I took care of him in an alleyway," he revealed.

The realization of what Daniel was saying showed on Sara's face, and her expression relaxed. "Are you suggesting," she inquired in a flat tone, looking her brother in the face, "that the bastard is *dead*?" Sara blinked and exhaled when she saw Dan nod in verification. "Crap." She inhaled. "Mom was telling the truth?" Sara's eyes widened, and tears flowed down her cheeks. She grabbed her crutches, using them for stability, and worked her way across the room to stare out the window to the surrounding neighborhood. A coat of fresh snow blanketed the ground. It had snowed the entire morning. Whirling to gaze at her brother, Sara grinned. "You want to know how I am still alive, big brother?" she asked, her lips drawn into a thin line. Sara smirked as she waited for her brother to acknowledge the question. Sara was, in fact, enjoying the look of bemusement on her brother's face. The question had obviously startled him.

It occurred to Daniel to ask, but he had declined to do so for some reason, unexplained to even him. He thought Sara would bring the subject up on her own, which she eventually had. "If you want to tell me, sis, please go ahead," he answered. Dan decided not to say anything else and just let her talk.

59

Sara turned back toward the window and hunched her shoulders. "Would you believe our *grandmother* is the one who deceived her son?" She smirked. "Leah watched him for years, pretending to instruct him. I don't give a damn if you realize this or not, but I'll tell you anyway. Leah was working with J. Edgar Hoover as an agent. She was copying everything the Saviano enterprise typed on paper and mailing it to Quantico. Dad thought he had figured it out, who the mole was, and set up a hit on one of his associates. The man he murdered was actually working with Leah, though. The man came up the evening before he was murdered and told us dad wanted to execute all of us. His name was Michael."

Daniel's eyes grew, recalling the man's name. "Do you mean the guy having the liaison with mom?" His jaw dropped. At his sister's questioning glance, Daniel explained, "I walked in on them the night before he perished." He frowned and finished, "I told dad about the relationship." He regretted his mistake even now. The fact was, he liked Michael Cromwell from the minute he saw him. Truthfully, it hadn't mattered to Daniel that Michael was sleeping with Patricia. Daniel told Jack about the encounter because he thought the knowledge would satisfy his dad, causing Jack to want to invest more time with him. This was the rationale of a teenager who needed nothing more than his father's blessing.

Sara scowled, nodding. "Yes, it was him. As I mentioned, he warned Leah, and Leah told Mom and me. I was too immature to understand. Remember I took a theater class in school my junior term? Well, thank God I did. With Leah's direction, we replaced the bullets in dad's gun with blanks without his knowledge. When he shot at mom, she made it appear he killed her, spreading pig blood everywhere. I did the same when he shot at me." Sara turned and scowled at Dan. Her eyes overflowed with a mixture of anger and anguish. "If you stayed rather than being a spineless coward, you would have noticed we were still alive."

At his sister's comments, Daniel hung his head. For a moment, words formed in his mind, yet he could not express them aloud. Moving closer, Dan placed a soft hand on Sara's shoulder and draped his arms around her in a hug. Sensing she didn't want to talk, he said nothing, merely held her to him. She was crying. Hot tears dampened the collar of his shirt. Daniel stroked her back, his palm moving up and down as her shoulders heaved.

After a while, Sara drew back, shifting to look through the window at the fluttering snow. "I'm sorry, Dan," she murmured. "I know you didn't realize what happened. If there was a way I could have warned you ahead of time . . ." She faltered in mid-sentence as she tried to breathe, her breast heaving from the unshed tears.

Daniel relaxed his grip on Sara's arm and gazed out the window. "It doesn't matter, Sara. What's important is that he's gone. Maybe we can go on with our lives now." He exhaled and ran a palm across his face. Noticing the discarded bag of food Sara dropped on the counter, her brother chuckled. "Short Stuff, are you going to eat that?"

he inquired, nodding toward the sack.

Sara looked at the food and then at Dan. "If you even consider touching that damn paper sack," she teased with a smirk, "you will meet an acquaintance of mine." She turned toward the bag, reached down, and jerked it from his grasp, sticking her tongue out at him.

Daniel chuckled. "Oh? And who might your friend be?" he inquired. His eyes sparkled, loving the cat-and-mouse game they were performing.

Sara blinked twice, considering her reply. "Well, let's just say you'll be walking with a limp for days, Dan," she answered, her eyes sharp with delight.

Dan smirked in response. Brushing off his sister's threat, he picked up the sack and drew out a glazed dough-nut. "Got coffee?" he asked, tasting the doughnut.

Sara laughed and seized the bag from him. "Yeah. It's in the break room across the corridor. I thought you'd come here after Mom called me last night." She smirked, produced a capped Styrofoam cup of cappuccino, and offered it to him.

Daniel removed the lid and drew a sip. He grinned in blessing. "Good cappuccino," he admitted. "Why don't we relax, Sara? There are still lots of factors we need to consider." Daniel sat on the couch, and his sister followed him. Her movements were stiffer than his, but at last, she sat beside him.

Once the pair made themselves comfortable, Daniel closed his eyes, reflecting. "How've you been?" he in-quired with apprehension. He opened his eyes and stretched his palms across his lap. "I should have called first, but . . . everything happened so quickly."

Sara scoffed at her brother, her eyebrows lifting in incredulity. "I guess that could be true. But it's been *twenty years* since we last saw each other." She did not specifically say what she was suggesting, but Daniel guessed from the look on her face that she wished everything had happened differently between them. Daniel had the impression that Sara had wanted him to find her after they were separated all those years ago. And during their conversation, he realized why. Dan learned from Sara that after she went to live with Aunt Janice, she had Sara institutionalized. But apparently, when Sara grew up, she was able to leave and live on her own.

Sara's time in the institution was not one she relished. The medical personnel took it upon themselves to use shock treatments and other horrific techniques. She had blocked out the men who raped her daily. But when the women had taken turns, she allowed them, and she found that she enjoyed the "treatments" as they were referred to.

"Look," Daniel said, slipping into what he called his detective method, "I understand why you're upset with me. I don't know what I hoped to accomplish by coming here. I guess I felt I owed it to you to explain what happened between Jack and me." He stood, and his shoulders arched. Scowling at his sister, he snapped, "You of all people should understand." He reached into his wallet, removed enough cash to provide for the pastries and coffee, and slapped the bills on Sara's lap. "Here you go, sis. This should compensate for the meal," he hissed.

Sara watched as her brother approached the exit to her office and sighed. "I was *resentful*, Danny." She dropped her eyes, staring at her palms. Sara was becoming weaker every day. She needed him more than ever, but her pride won the internal argument. Sara reached for her crutches and stood up shakily on them, momentarily losing her balance. She stepped toward her brother. He twisted to meet her, and she looked him straight in the eye.

Dan noticed Sara's momentary loss of equilibrium and was by her side in seconds. "Tell me the truth, Sara. How are you?" he demanded. Dan needed to hear the truth to confirm his suspicions. He ushered her backward to the sofa, and she fell against the cushion, muttering in revulsion. Crouching beside her, he patted her knee gently.

To Sara, her brother's words seemed patronizing, but she said nothing. She scowled. "Oh, Danny Boy, that is the million-dollar question." Spreading her palms across her lap, she gazed at her brother. She could no longer hide her emotions, despite her best efforts. Tears appeared in the corners of her eyes, and she sobbed out, "I'm dying."

Chapter 12

The Past

Jack stared at the physician seated on the opposite side of the mahogany desk, steepled his fingers to his lips, and spoke. "Are you insinuating, Doctor Harrison, that my girl will *die*?" He arched a skeptical eyebrow at the crimson-haired man and contemplated the doctor's next words, expecting a grim answer.

The doctor leaned across his desk, his ice-blue eyes sparkling. "It is definitely a possibility, Mr. Saviano. The tests my partners and I ran came back positive for the neurological condition hydrocephalus. It is doubtful Sara will walk or talk if she even survives that long. Even more so, she will have weak muscles and varying cognitive disabilities. My recommendation, sir and madam," he nodded in Patricia's direction, at last giving her acknowledgment, "is that you end her existence *now* before you become passionately affected." He did not add that Sara's survival chances would eventually decrease to nothing, even with adequate medical care. For her to thrive, it would take a miracle.

Jack stood abruptly, his hands curled into tight fists.

He scowled at the other man and hissed, "The answer is *no*. I *demand* my child survive. To end my own daughter's existence is not possible." With those remarks, Jack whirled on his heel and headed toward the exit. "Let's leave, Pat." He snarled and left the room, not waiting for her to acknowledge the command.

Patricia rose slowly, gathering her purse and gloves, waiting until her partner was out of earshot. She glanced at the doctor and declared: "Everything must play out until the last act, Dennis."

Dennis Harrison placed a palm on Patricia's arm. Lowering his voice, he answered, "I don't see how long I can continue with this farce, Pat. Jack will eventually discover Sara is not his daughter. What will you do?"

From the other room, Jack growled impatiently, "I said let's get the hell out of here, Pat!" He muttered something about suing the doctor for misdiagnosis. Nodding in understanding, Patricia refused to comment and left the office.

When Patricia had completely disappeared, Dennis crossed the room to his desk and seized the phone. Making a call, he paused a few seconds, and when the individual on the other end answered, he declared, "It's a go." With those words, he hung up the phone and leaned back in his chair, hiding his face with his palms. The man who Patricia called an ally for years wept and screamed.

Once Dennis regained his composure, he opened a drawer and removed a letter-sized envelope. He addressed it and set it on the desk. Dennis pulled out a handgun from the same drawer. The man held the barrel between his lips, fingers trembling. He mumbled a prayer, then whispered, "Forgive me." With a sob, Dennis pulled the trigger, ending his life.

Chapter 13

The Present

Daniel looked at his sister, his eyes wide with alarm. He laid his left hand on the girl's knee. "What do you mean, Sara?" He uttered the question.

When his sister answered, her words held a trace of pain. "My hydrocephalus is worsening, Dan," she mumbled. "Over the last four weeks, I've been suffering excruciating headaches and intense nausea, and my balance is failing. My doctors say it won't be long before I am dead."

Daniel opened his mouth to comfort Sara but then promptly shut it. He recalled learning about treatments. A shunt, or catheter, drained fluid from the brain to the abdomen. It was not a complete, foolproof cure, however, as sometimes shunts failed. They had to be replaced in case of a malfunction. How could he reassure her that treatment was available? Words escaped his mind. He rose and went to the desk and looked at the family pictures again. His shoulders sagged, and he puffed out a moan. "What can I do, sis?" he offered, not turning. He couldn't bear to face her and see the tears appearing in the corners of her eyes. Dan couldn't stand for her to see his tears, either.

Sara took her crutches and made her way to where her brother stood. She pulled out an envelope from inside her coat and gave it to him. "The answer to your question, brother, dear, is in this envelope," she murmured, closing her eyes as she waited.

Daniel tore open the envelope and removed the single piece of stationery. Once he scanned the letter, he pivoted to stare at Sara. At the movement, Sara lost her stability, but she corrected herself. "No, God dammit. No!" Dan wheezed, brandishing the letter in the air. The document described how Sara preferred to die, when, and where. A physician and several lawyers had certified it. Daniel assumed Sara asked someone in her law firm to help her write out the paperwork.

"You have no option, Danny," Sara retorted. "Kill me. You owe me as much." She hesitated, softening her tone and concluding, "Or, more to the point, help me kill myself."

Daniel turned toward a recliner, his knees bending as he dropped into the leather. God knew he was at a loss for words. He expected several scenarios playing out once he discovered his sister, but *this* was the last one he expected. "No," he said again, exhaling with his eyes wide in alarm. They briefly closed, then snapped back open as they clouded with tears. "I *won't*," he asserted.

Sara glowered at him. Taking the letter from him and tossing it aside with a glare, she growled, "I expected you would do it and not argue with me! But you are *still* a coward, aren't you?"

Chapter 14

The Past

Patricia sat in her living room, her hands protecting her face, masking her whimpers. She had learned of Dennis's suicide. The detectives interrogated her so persistently, she nearly errantly confessed to shooting him. Only the postmortem revealed he committed suicide.

Brushing at her eyes to obscure the anguish in her heart, Patricia picked up her mug of coffee with quivering hands. She stared at the dark liquid and bit her bottom lip so hard it brought blood. Loosening the cup from its death grip, Patricia's eyes drifted toward the bloodstained envelope. In Dennis's familiar handwriting across the top of the pale white envelope was Patricia's name.

Why, Patricia thought, *did he send me this?* What was in it that wasn't something he could have shared with her hours earlier? Her hands trembling, Patricia tore the envelope open as she reflected on how it came to be in her possession. Dennis's contact at the police station—the person he called—came to collect it and deliver it to her before the rest of the police arrived at the scene, according to Dennis's explicit instructions. It was the plan Dennis prearranged for if he ever thought Jack suspected that Sara was not his daughter. Dennis's friend carried it out flawlessly, unbeknownst to his law enforcement colleagues.

Patricia read the paper then angrily crushed it. In Dennis's suicide note, he explained that he could no longer live with the anxiety of keeping Sara's real father a secret from Jack, who he was sure would kill him when he found out. Dennis was her ally and adviser for many years. He was the one man who would have and could have helped her raise Sara. Now he was dead, and her heart ached. Patricia had never hated Jack more.

Chapter 15

The Present

Sara Saviano whimpered in horror. She was losing her strength. After learning the facts behind who her real parents were years ago, she felt a sense of disappointment and deception. But Daniel was to learn nothing more about what went on in their family other than what he had already learned. Sara had promised Leah that and had no option, or else Leah would make her suffer. *Damn Leah for learning the truth about my health, and damn her for blackmailing me into silence over it*, Sara thought.

Leah had discovered that Sara was actually in far better health than she let on, and she used that wisdom to compel the younger woman into fooling her half-brother, making him believe she was dying. The irony of discovering the truth is that you can blackmail those who don't wish it known.

As Daniel's glazed stare penetrated her soul, Sara understood he was so absorbed in thought that he didn't even notice her anymore. Though curious about the thoughts troubling her brother's mind so profoundly, she discovered she was too frightened to urge him to share.

Resigned, Sara released a moan as she braced her elbows on the windowsill. She looked at the scenery in silence.

The revelation that Sara wanted Daniel to help her die was, in his eyes, an incomprehensible one. Sara had already predicted her brother would try everything in his capacity to escape fulfilling the demand. If Leah's plan was going to work, though, Sara needed to continue the ruse. "Dan," she sighed, "I am miserable. The agony I experience is intolerable. I know the circumstances of the previous several hours have been difficult for you. I am certain what is going on is painful to comprehend. But as dad often quoted, 'the grass is always greener where the shit drops.'"

Daniel laughed, thinking of several occasions when his dad said those exact words. He laid his palm on his sister's shoulder, squeezing it. Then, he rested the palm on hers. "I suppose he had his positive qualities," he noted. Jack's sense of humor was one of his most appealing aspects.

Sara nodded in agreement. Then, she stood. Daniel stared in amazement as the dark-haired woman moved remarkably fast to her desk and plunked into her leather armchair. Her head shot up as she understood too late the mistake she made. Sara swallowed hard and growled under her breath, swearing furiously. "Dammit to Hell," she muttered, her eyes shutting as she chewed her bottom lip. She struggled to brush off her mistake. Regaining her dignity, she reopened her eyes and plucked a thin gray envelope from the corner of her desk. She hurled it across the office. "Someone left this for you," she informed Dan, her eyes glowing in a sudden rage.

Daniel continued to stare at Sara. His brain did not register what transpired. He finally took the envelope from the floor and tore it open. He unfolded the sheet, staring at the contents: *Meet me where it started. I have the answers to your questions.* It was unsigned and was dated the day before. Dan studied his sister, arching his eyebrow, but he received no answers.

* * *

Jack opened his eyes, flinching with the effort. He blinked once, twice, and a third time. "Where am I?" he asked himself aloud. Darkness enveloped him, but instinct told him it was daytime. Getting up, he tried to figure out where he was and how long he had been there. A glimmer of memory invaded his brain, and he rubbed the spot on his rib cage where the bullet punctured his skin.

"Shit!" He growled the word with an expression that would have made his mother blush, adding, "The witch who shot me will pay." He had survived, which was a miracle. *How did he?* It was a question without an obvious answer, at least to the naked eye. The bullet had only grazed his breast but far enough into the skin that he had passed out from shock and that blood had pooled as it flowed around the wound, making it look far worse than it was. Jack remembered that the last thing he saw before fully losing consciousness was the form of his son crawling through the snow toward him. But Jack had also glimpsed the face of the turncoat who tried to send him to Hell—not Daniel, but *Leah*! She had stayed concealed by shadows to Daniel, but Jack had an excellent view from where he was.

Before Jack passed out a second time, he mumbled profanity against his offspring and the other individual who deceived him that night: "Burn in Hell, Leah, and suffer excruciating torment!"

Hours later, Jack turned, and a wail of sorrow escaped his lips. He thought again about what happened. Opening his eyes, Jack scrutinized his surroundings. As he became more used to the light, he realized he was no longer alone. He saw someone leaning against a wall, watching him, and he knew he was no longer where he had been the last time he awoke. His mouth was dry, prohibiting him from trying to communicate. At last, he was able to ask, "Where am I? Who are you?"

The figure turned toward him, and Jack could see it was a girl dressed in ragged clothes. She looked down at Jack and kneeled beside him. "You're in a deserted warehouse," the blonde-haired girl explained. "I discovered you in a garbage bin just before daybreak, realized somebody shot you, and brought you here. Then, I treated your wounds. I was a nursing graduate, so I knew what to do." In her palm, she grasped a bottle of water. She opened it and presented it to Jack.

Raising his head, Jack took a cautious sip. He nudged the bottle aside and shook his head. He rose, bracing against the wall to help him regain his stability. Drawing a sharp gasp, the mobster shuddered. Examining the place, he took in the scene of an abandoned factory: the rubbish of boxes, papers, and metal frames of old equipment. He shuffled and peered at the girl standing beside him, and he realized she would recognize him if she saw him again. He sensed she had gone through his pockets, probably searching for cash and identification. He also realized that his crucifix was missing and assumed she must have taken it.

Jack needed to dispose of her. How could he take care of it without drawing anyone's attention? Looking around once more, he saw an open medical kit. He inquired if the girl had any sedatives. She said, "yes." The woman shifted and strode toward a cardboard box. As she did, Jack matched her pace, and before she knew what happened, he grabbed her. One hand covered her mouth to stop her from shouting. She struggled, trying to escape from his grip, but it was hopeless. In one unexpected move, he twisted her neck. There was a loud crack as the bones split under pressure, and she crumpled lifelessly at his feet.

Jack squinted at the body resting there. "Thanks," he whispered through clenched teeth as he pulled the vial from her fingers and turned to walk away. She did a perfect job on his chest wound. The blood stopped flowing. He needed to go home, shower, and dispose of the clothes he now wore or risk exposure.

* * *

77

"**H**ey, Dan," Roger Wilson called from where he kneeled in the far corner of the dimly-lit warehouse. "Looks like we got a fresh one." Twenty years after they left Canada, Roger's wife and young child perished in a bus accident. He later learned that the negligence of the bus company had caused the accident. Inspired by his grief, Roger graduated from the local medical school with honors and became a medical examiner.

Roger laughed at his statement, which he appeared to think was the funniest joke on Earth. Noting that Dan was far from amused, he continued. "From witness accounts, I would guess she's been dead four hours. A warehouse 'resident' discovered her after showing up here searching for a woman known around here as 'Doc.' Apparently, she was a nurse at one time." As he talked, he examined the body for lacerations or visible scars.

Creasing his eyebrow in thought, Daniel seemed surprised. "A nurse? She hardly looks old enough to be a teenager." He kneeled with gloved hands and poked and examined the deceased woman's form. Her light-brown eyes were now barren, staring at nothing. Daniel found himself attracted to her eyes but was unsure why. They looked familiar to him, as though he knew her. But the sense of déjà vu faded.

Dan noticed bruises around the young girl's collar and larynx. He saw more on her right shoulder. But the shoulder bruises had been there for weeks, he guessed. Roger would know for sure. He made a note of the bruises and injuries. Arching his eyebrow, he glanced at Roger. "Are theses shoulder bruises P.M.?" he asked, using the abbreviation for "postmortem." Dan needed to know if they occurred before or after the girl died. His eyes moved back to the wounds.

Roger groaned a little as he faced Dan. Shaking his head, he answered, "Nope, *peri*mortem. They are from an earlier assault." Turning his focus to what he was doing, he examined the young girl's collar with his gloved fingers. "I'd say in the last week or so."

Daniel was sad to know she had suffered so much, and he muttered a four-letter word. "Did you do a rape kit yet?" The victim seemed to show no signs of rape, though. Peering down at the body and the impassive face with sightless light-brown eyes, he suddenly recognized her. "Sandy," Daniel muttered in horror. Sandra Blake was Sara's best friend throughout their junior and high school years. She was one of Sara's aides for a brief time while in high school. Despite his shame over her ailments, Jack had allowed Sara to attend school, but he otherwise kept her restricted to her room. Sara's condition embarrassed him.

"No." Roger shook his head and went on. "From my preliminary exam, she wasn't raped. But when we return to the morgue, I'll be able to complete a more detailed examination," Roger explained. He noticed the look of recognition on his colleague's face. "What is it?"

Daniel waved his hand dismissively. "I thought I recognized the victim. Hey, Roger? Do me a favor, okay?" At the man's questioning glance, Daniel finished, "Take care of her. She isn't some unidentified vagrant." He considered his sister as he spoke, and how he would act if something like this happened to her. He turned away from the medical examiner and skimmed the area with his naked eye, noticing nothing out of the ordinary. Then, he grabbed a few items from the handbag he brought with him.

Daniel searched the area using ultraviolet light and luminol. He looked for anything that might reveal the identity of Sandra's killer or a motive. He detected no blood or semen stains. The place was clean. What caught his eye was a narrow strip of gauze lying a few feet away from a sleeping bag. He dropped the bandage into a Ziploc bag, securing it, and kneeled to inspect the sleeping bag. "Get this to the lab." He handed the packet with the gauze strips in it over to Roger.

The medical examiner promised to get the evidence to the lab when they had concluded at the crime scene. Directing one of his aides to put the sleeping bag in a plastic sack, he gestured to Daniel. "Anything else I can do for you?" he spat, his accent thick in his tone. He was exhausted and annoyed.

Daniel peered at his friend briefly and wrung his hands nervously. "No. Just call me after you complete the postmortem. I also need a photocopy of the results on my desk as quickly as workable." He peeked at his watch. Darkness would arrive shortly. It had been a long, agonizing day, and he covered his mouth to suppress a loud yawn. He was ready to go home.

Roger nodded in agreement. "Will do," he replied, turning to one of his assistants. "Let's get the hell out of here, Will," the coroner continued, disposing of his examination gloves. Skimming the area, he looked once more at Daniel and grimaced. "Get some sleep, Dan." He sighed, acknowledging how gaunt and fatigued Daniel looked. "Everything will be clearer in the morning." He disappeared with a slight wave of his hand. "I'll call you as soon as I finish the autopsy," Roger called over his shoulder.

Daniel turned back toward the spot where the body had been only minutes before. Something odd caught his view. Squatting down, Daniel lowered his eyes to a place a few inches from the chalk outline. A needle and syringe lay in the center of the outline, alongside some blood spatter. Sliding the syringe into another evidence bag, he drew a sample of the blood. Something else bugged him, but he could not place what it was. He grunted, rubbing the bridge of his nose. Daniel turned from the scene and leaned against a wall. He closed his eyes, groaning, and then reopened them.

Not having time to drop the additional evidence off at his office, Daniel stripped off his rubber gloves and put the evidence in his coat pocket. He made sure the crime scene was secure, locked the warehouse door, and turned toward his car. Yawning, he unlocked the car door and crumpled into the driver's seat. Dan drove to his condominium. As he sought to stay alert, Daniel never detected a van pull away and trail after him. It was the same van that had trailed him the night he thought he had killed Jack.

Arriving at his apartment, Daniel stepped out of his sedan. Locking it, he walked to the front door. He fumbled with his keys before dropping them. The cacophony of metal hitting concrete rattled his nerves and made him jump. Stooping to pick the keys up, he felt eyes watching him. Turning, he peered up and down the pavement. His tired mind registered the van parked across the road, but he dismissed it as nothing.

Dan opened the door to his apartment and continued inside, dropping the keys on the counter near the door. He went into the kitchen and turned on his coffee maker. As sleepy as he was, Dan needed a hot drink. Moving to the kitchen counter, Dan removed his coat and went through the pockets, emptying them of the contents. He knew it was against protocol to take evidence home, but he thought it was safer with him.

Hanging the coat over the back of an armchair, Dan poured hot cocoa. He picked up the bags of evidence, went into his bedroom, and set the cocoa mug on his nightstand. Opening a drawer, he dropped the evidence inside and closed it, locking it with a key. He then sat on his bed, picked up the mug, and took a sip. He next headed to the bathroom, where he turned on the hot water valve and stripped off his clothes. He climbed inside to have a shower, letting the steamy water cascade over his fatigued and throbbing frame.

At last, Dan emerged from the shower, opened a large

bath towel, draped it around his abdomen, and came back to the bedroom. Toweling dry, he drew on a pair of boxers and slid into bed, then settled back, letting his tired muscles relax before shifting and turning off the light. Daniel tossed and turned, his mind in overdrive, as he tried to fall asleep. Faces and names flashed in and out of his subconscious as questions whirled around his brain. But within minutes, he was deeply asleep.

Chapter 16

The Past

Jack opened the door and saw something that made his blood turn cold. The couple had not noticed him enter. "Patricia? What's going on?" he bellowed. His eyes narrowed in fury. He stood in the den, pointing in amazement at the fellow sitting next to her on the couch. A surprised Andrew Davenport glared at both of them. Jack said nothing else. The pair were in each other's arms.

"I . . . I . . . that is . . . we . . ." Patricia was stammering idiotically. Breaking free of the embrace, she felt like an idiot, too. It wasn't because she had her pants down but because she was with one of Jack's best friends. Her palm brushed against Andrew's, instructing him to stay silent. He recognized the unspoken hint and closed his mouth.

Jack growled at Andrew. "Don't move, you son of a bitch!" He crossed the room. Jack grabbed his spouse by her arm so hard she shrieked in anguish as she struggled against him. Directing her to stand, Jack all but jerked her to the other side of the den. He shoved her to the floor. When she landed, he pressed his knee into the center of her back, holding her in place. There was no escape for her, and Patricia tried to keep from howling in agony. "I have a thought, Andrew!" Jack declared over his shoulder. Sneering, he drew out a revolver from under his coat. He aimed it at the base of his wife's scalp, cocking the weapon. "Why don't I make you watch your lover *die*?"

Andrew opened his eyes, studying Jack. "What the hell?" he demanded in horror. Time stopped in an instant. He held his breath and then said what popped into his brain. "Jesus Christ, what is going on?"

Jack scowled at the man he called his friend. "Answer me by God!" he exploded, brandishing the weapon in the air. He asked, with an eerie calm, "Do you choose your lover to perish?"

Before Andrew could respond, Patricia squirmed, gagging. The pressure on her back was unbearable. She couldn't inhale, and Jack knew he was hurting her. He was boasting as he thrust the handgun harder into the back of her neck. Jack cocked the gun. Not repeating the query, Jack gave Patricia the impression that he would execute her if she said nothing. "Jack," she sighed his name like a prayer, "please, I implore you, don't harm the kids. Kill me if you must, but for God's sake, don't hurt Sara or Daniel." Tears streamed from her eyes as she gagged on the words.

Jack scowled at the man who was screwing his spouse. Sneering, he stated, "Your luck's run out, jackass. I am a compassionate person, so I will offer you an alternative, Andrew. Does Patricia die, or will it be you?" He cocked his head, gesturing from Andrew to Patricia and back.

Still on the floor, Patricia turned her head to peer at Andrew. "Don't," she pleaded. Coughing, she gulped the bile appearing in her throat. She was advising him to let her perish. Once it happened, everything would be all right. Patricia had an unconquerable determination and an even more definite conviction in God than she realized.

A soft, frightened voice interrupted the trio before Jack could fire the gun. "Dad? Mom? What's going on here?" Both of Jack Saviano's children stood in the doorway, their mouths open wide in terror.

Jack turned toward the sound of his boy's voice, his gun hand rising away from Patricia. He cursed and mumbled under his breath. Suddenly, he pointed the gun back at his spouse and yelled, "Die!"

The room's other door flew open, and Leah stood there, her eyes tight in contempt. "Not tonight, Jackie Boy!" she spat. Pulling out her firearm, she kept her aim at Jack. As the gun discharged, Andrew sprang to his feet to shield his friend, even though Jack had threatened to execute him moments earlier. The slug hit Andrew. He dropped to his knees as blood spewed from the wound in his heart. Hitting the floor, seemingly in slow motion, Andrew let out a soft exclamation of astonishment, and his eyes rolled in his skull as he took his last breath.

Patricia froze in horror as Jack turned toward her, scorn written all over his face. Raising the handgun in his fist, he pulled the trigger. A sneer of satisfaction touched the corners of his mouth, and she shrieked as the projectile seemed to strike her.

Facing his children, Jack screamed a severe warning at them: "Run before I execute you, too." His children stood frozen, shaken by what they witnessed moments before. Their mother lay comatose in a widening puddle of crimson blood.

Jack raised the handgun and aimed it at Sara, firing another round, thinking his aim was true. As he did, the children ran. Daniel took his sister around her shoulders, almost catapulting her toward the front door of the mansion. Their bodies shook with fright, and Daniel almost slipped in blood that he assumed was coming from Sara. The blood followed them as he steered his distraught sister outside.

Once outside, Daniel released Sara from his grip and lowered her to the ground. To his astonishment, several people attired in black suits hurried over to them. They squatted in front of the pair, signaling for them to sit. He did as directed, and the shock he experienced moments earlier substituted with confusion. "Who are you? What's going on?" He glanced first at his sister and then at them. "Hey! Leave her alone!" he shouted as he saw one man was speaking to Sara.

"It's alright, son," the person said, glancing at him. "I'm a colleague of Leah's. Everything will be fine." His manner was comforting, even though there was a rough edge to it. An Irish brogue echoed in his pitch. "My name is Agent Donovan. But you may call me Sean," he finished. "Your sister is a little shaken up, but she will be all right."

"I am not your son, mister," Daniel grunted, jerking away. He swallowed and took a sharp breath. Softening his tone, he continued, "Please explain what is going on here. Who are you? Why is Leah here? Why did she try to kill my father?" The questions tumbled from his mouth.

Dan was impatient, waiting to hear the answers. His shoulders sank as he demanded them, and he felt exhausted. Daniel felt vulnerable, and he detested the feeling. "I'm sorry," he apologized, "I am upset." He closed his eyes, took a shaky breath, and then reopened them, staring at Sean and seeing him clearly for the first time.

Sean leaned back on his heels to inspect the children. *What could he tell Daniel?* He knew the answers, but he believed it wasn't his call to provide them. "Tell you what, Danny," he murmured after a minute. "Why don't we take you and your sister somewhere warm? You must be hungry."

Daniel reached his palm toward his sister, bringing her closer to him. He knew she was frightened. Her frame trembled against his and she was whimpering. Her fists clenched his shirt. "It's okay," he soothed. Glancing at Sean, he nodded once in agreement. His belly rumbled at the prospect of food, and for the first time, he grinned. "That sounds wonderful," he whispered, nodding to his sister. "Short Stuff? Are you hungry?" he inquired.

His sister nodded. "Yeah, let's go," she answered, squinting at the guy in the black suit. The trio did not glance back at the quiet house as they shuffled to an awaiting car. If they had, they would have seen Jack Saviano standing on the front balcony, witnessing his family taken away from him. Leah stood next to him, her palm resting on his arm. Offering a silent prayer of thanks, she ushered Jack away. It would be the last time his children were together.

Chapter 17

The Present

Sweat poured off Daniel's anxious body, and he awoke with a start. Sitting bolt upright in bed, Daniel scanned the surrounding area. Something seemed amiss. Someone else was in the apartment. He reached grabbed his pistol, slid out of bed, and shuffled across the floor to the door.

Allowing his eyes to become accustomed to the dark, Dan moved around the apartment. Going from the bedroom through every room, he saw nothing out of place. Running his palm through his hair with his free hand, he went back to his bed. The memories he thought he had buried decades ago returned. Sean Donovan had been a comfort to the Saviano children, and Daniel wondered if the agent was still alive. Daniel resolved to call Leah in the morning and inquire whether she still knew anything about the man.

Something was still wrong. The hairs on Dan's neck rose. But he was sure it was just tiredness causing him to think this way. Again, he went to the kitchen and flipped on the switch. Bright light saturated the kitchen, and he looked around. Everything was fine. Moving to the coffee maker, he used it to make another cup of hot chocolate. Taking a sip of the hot liquid, he twisted and strode to the counter. Rubbing his face, he stared down at the chair. His coat was missing. Where did it go? He recalled leaving it there before having his shower and retiring to bed. Who had taken it, and why?

Memories of the trip home flashed through his mind. He recalled seeing the van parked out on the road. "Who is it, and why would they be there?" he wondered. Then, he remembered the evidence he had placed in his coat pocket. Someone was after it! Dan came back to the bedroom. Pushing the door open, he turned on the light and stopped in his tracks. The drawer to his nightstand was ajar, its contents exposed. The evidence had vanished! Someone was trying to erase any trace that might connect them to the crime scene.

Daniel felt his knees bend, barely understanding what had transpired. How had they gained entrance to his residence and gotten the evidence? He was positive he latched the lock when he arrived home. Moving toward the front door, he gripped the doorknob and twisted it. The door swung open. Groaning with disgust, he growled, "Dammit, I'm a cop, for God's sake! Why would I be so foolish not to lock my front door?" Locking it, he returned to the bedroom.

He dressed at a snail's pace. Rubbing his eyes, he slipped his gun under his black jacket. His shift started in less than an hour, and he hoped to get there before his co-workers got the better pastries. Glancing around, he noted the light on his answering machine was flashing. Crossing the apartment, he pressed the "play" button. His face paled as the delicate voice rang throughout the room: "You thought you knew it all. Well, I have news for you: you will realize when I'm finished with you how to die! I told you to meet me where it all began."

It was six o'clock when Daniel stepped into his police station. At half-past the hour, he was pouring over years of unsettled murder cases. Leaning back, his mind drifted to the weeks before his meeting with his dad. Leah called him without warning and informed him she had watched him and his father for the last forty years. She claimed she kept a carton containing documentation that she and Detective Weldon Keyes had been working on together during that period. Leah told Daniel she would give him the files, which she did. The murder cases were among them.

Each of the unsolved murder cases Daniel reviewed had, he believed, a similar modus operandi to the one involved in Sandy's death, all involving victims with sliced or crushed throats. Forty-six cases, all having the same or similar M.O.

Daniel entered the resident FBI website. There, he discovered that W. Keyes had been an agent for twenty years and had been Leah's colleague for ten. His history of obtaining convictions, not unlike Leah's, was flawless. According to the "official" story, Keyes took early retirement, having become worn out by the murder cases. But the unauthorized version, according to an undisclosed source, was that Keyes was forced into a new job. It happened just two days shy of him planning to arrest the one man he suspected in the unsolved murders: Jack Saviano.

Chapter 18

The Past

"**Y**ou feel so wonderful, baby." The murderer whispered the words into the girl's ear like a prayer. A small gasp escaped the killer's throat, and for a split second, the victim tried to breathe. After a long minute, she sat upright.

The girl uttered a quiet, "Thank you, darling," and she braced her palm under her chin, rolling on her side to inspect her mate. "You know, you're . . . extraordinary." A murmur of delight escaped her lips. "It's been so long since I've been held like this. Not since I learned what it meant to be in love and have someone make love to me."

At the words, the other person opened their mouth to say something but then closed it. When they could recover their voice, they inquired, "You're *in love* with me?" A weak laugh escaped their lips. "I don't understand. We agreed, Monica, when we first did this that there would be nothing more than sex! And now you're telling me you have *feelings* for me?" The person snorted. "No, I can't allow this to continue."

"What?! What are you suggesting, baby? I love you!" Monica's lips quivered, and she prayed she wouldn't break down. She knew her lover detested any hints of vulnerability, and crying was one such display.

"Oh, you know exactly what I am saying. It was fun while it lasted, but now . . . I'm sorry, it's over between us. Go. Leave." The words were brusque and laced with hatred. The figure stood and, shoving Monica aside, grabbed her clothes and hurled them at her. But the clothes missed their target and fell inches away.

"Why? Did I do something wrong?" The radical shift in her suitor surprised the girl. Shaking, Monica struggled to take her clothes that were in a heap on the floor. Hooking her foot in them, she stumbled and fell facedown, knocking the wind out of her trembling body.

The mysterious figure was now shaking with an uncontrollable rage Monica had never seen before. "I begged you to leave!" Monica's lover stood over her in the next instant, eyes glaring. "You should have listened!" they said, snarling. The knife plunged into Monica's throat and downward toward her chest. Monica's screams echoed through the entire house and then fell silent as the murderer finished their grisly work.

The killer's second victim, somewhat similar to Monica, surrendered her life via a crushed larynx. She was naked, her genitals were drenched in blood, and her right nipple had been bitten. The killer had eviscerated the young girl's body, and the girl's face was no longer recognizable. Only a coroner could identify the corpse.

During the next several weeks, the police would confirm the corpse as Lucy Cowlings. She was the offspring of Darren and Myra Cowlings. Her mom would later say she hoped and prayed her daughter's murderer would rot in Hell. "No mercy for the asshole!" she insisted. Lucy's dad held the same opinion as his wife. It was well-known Darren was a staff member of Thomas Anderson who had "contacts." Thomas would make sure Lucy had justice.

Chapter 19

The Present

Blood once again pooled from the wound in the center of Jack's rib cage. He struggled to run, and his feet appeared rooted to the ground. *So, this is how I die? What rotten luck I have! First, my son wants to turn me in. Then, I discover my mother wishes to execute me!* The thoughts faded, and Jack sank once more into oblivion.

* * *

Daniel shoved the chair he was resting on aside and rose. Groaning, he stretched and felt several bones in his spine snap. Glancing at the wall clock above him, Dan had less than an hour before his strange encounter was to occur. "Where it all began," he mumbled under his breath, recounting the instructions from the note Sara had given him and from the message on his answering machine. Dan's instinct told him the location was the alleyway where he encountered his father. But the more he contemplated it, he realized the note referred to his childhood home. The problem was that the present owners had already told him they didn't want him there. He was a member of the despised Saviano family and therefore a trespasser. *How*, he wondered, *am I supposed to get in?*

It occurred to Daniel that after he and his family left the home, the new owners—who still lived there—had installed a burglar alarm. There were various reports from their precinct that the alarm had been going off for no discernible reason. He knew this to be a fact because Frank Watkins, the security company owner and a friend of Daniel's, maintained the alarm system and confirmed it. It sounded odd to Daniel that the alarm would have issues. He called Frank to find out why the signal was performing erratically. He asked Frank to let him see the home.

At first, Frank hesitated, knowing it was against protocol. But since he was aware Daniel once occupied the home, he agreed to let him join. "Let me make certain everything is adequate with the Hamiltons," he cautioned. Frank encouraged the retired couple to go ahead with their vacation. He reminded them that New Zealand was beginning its summer, and if they put off their trip any longer, it would be too hot.

"They're leaving tomorrow at six in the morning," Frank informed Daniel on the phone half an hour after he had confirmed everything with Margie Hamilton. "I informed them I would stop by the house at ten to six so they could make sure they set the alarm beforehand. It will take no time to shut the alarm off once they leave." He smiled. "I'll have it corrected in ten minutes, and then the house is yours." Frank hesitated. "Are you positive about this? I realize it won't be easy for you to return there."

Daniel considered his answer for a minute. "Yes, Frank. I must do it. If I don't . . ." He let the sentence hang in midair.

"I understand, Dan." Frank hung up the phone after a few more last-minute arrangements and then leaned back in his recliner. He hoped for his friend's sake everything would work according to plan. A sudden chill went down his spine. Frank had the idea that Daniel wasn't telling him everything. Shrugging off the prophetic feeling, he carried out the arrangements.

The following morning, Daniel was awake and showered by four-thirty. He dressed and was at Frank's office within an hour. "There's no backing out now," Dan told himself once he and Frank were on the way to the Hamilton's. He ran his palm along his plum-colored coat and fingered the small pistol holstered there.

"We're here, Dan," Frank announced, nodding toward the mansion as he turned off the motor. He met and maintained his old friend's gaze for a long time. This was Dan's rodeo from then on. Frank knew Dan would prefer no further intrusion from him.

Daniel grinned and then removed his jacket and tie. Underneath the coat, he wore a uniform matching Frank's. Slipping the gun and holster free, he reached for Frank's toolbox on the floor. He opened the box, slipped both items inside the concealed compartment, shut the lid, and picked it up. The pair left the van, locking the doors behind them, and made their way to the front gate.

"Remember, you're my partner, Jeff. You're new on the job. I hired you the day before yesterday." Frank reminded Dan of his alias. Then, he snickered, looking at Dan. "You look ridiculous without your mustache." Daniel had shaved it off to change his appearance, although the uniform and baseball cap he wore hid any significant features anyway. Frank made sure Daniel had a spare key to the front and rear door if something went awry and he got locked out.

The Hamiltons were gone. Frank unlocked the door and went inside with Daniel. The switchboard for the alarm was in a small hallway closet. Frank opened the switchboard door, turned off the alarm, and checked everything that might make the alarm system malfunction. Frank knew the Hamiltons would be away at least three weeks, so he was in no rush to correct the issue. This would allow Dan to take his time searching around the mansion.

As Daniel stayed with his friend in the grand entrance, a wave of wistfulness came over him. It was such a great feeling as images from his childhood came rushing back to him. Walking a few paces, he noted how different the old place looked and felt, with shiny new shutters, sparkling silver walls, and smooth wood furniture. It had changed so much in the hands of the present owners!

Daniel wandered into the dining area. Pausing for a moment at the entrance, he imagined his family eating their evening meal. He recalled saying Grace before eating, and they always kept conversation to a minimum.

Once the meals were over, his mother would clear away the dishes, and he would go into the kitchen to help her wash them. His dad would go to his study after they brought his sister to bed.

Continuing on his way through the house, Dan came to the door that had been his bedroom. He grabbed the doorknob. Turning it, he pushed the door open, releasing it so it swung open on well-greased hinges. Swallowing hard, he went inside. Dan scanned the surrounding space. He imagined his bed, the armchair, and the modest desk where he completed his homework. The Hamiltons had not changed the appearance much, except for a different coat of paint, new draperies, and shag carpet. Turning and peeking behind a door, Dan inspected the closet where his clothes always hung. They had kept it. He vividly recalled his discovery of the loose panel in the closet's rear . . .

Having discovered the panel earlier in the day, young Daniel returned to the closet after everyone was asleep. There must be a way to free the panel, he thought. He remembered he had a penknife hidden in a drawer. He returned to the closet with it. He slipped the knife along one edge of the loose board, easing it toward him. The panel fell loose in his palms. The opening was deep enough for him to move through it.

Turning on a flashlight, Daniel swung it around the opening, discovering a chamber. He pressed through the hole and stepped onto a concrete floor. Turning the beam back and forth, he saw a table and an armchair in one corner. A single lightbulb hung from the ceiling. Shelves adorned the walls, and they held what appeared to be folders containing documents. Who would use this area? he wondered. Curiosity filled young Daniel's mind, and he was impatient to see more but knew time was against him. He realized he had to go to sleep because he had school and exams the next day.

When Daniel completed his tests the next day, he recalled, *he came back home, had dinner, and washed up. He retired to his room. Instead of looking at his homework, he returned to the closet to search once more. Swinging the light around the chamber he had discovered, Daniel was mindful not to disturb anything. As he explored, something caught his eye.*

Moving toward the table, Daniel stepped past it. In the corner behind it, he was sure he saw a sliver of illumination. On closer investigation, it appeared to be coming from the other side of the wall. Where did it come from or go? His mind swirled with a thousand questions. Overcome by curiosity, he ran his fingers up and down the surface where the light was originating. Squatting, his fingers rubbed against a slight indent in the wall. Turning on his heel, he gazed back over his shoulder. Holding his breath, Dan strained to pick up any noises that might reveal someone had discovered what he was doing.

Feeling sure he was alone, young Daniel laid his palm on the notch and pushed against the wall. To his shock, it moved sideways to present a recognizable area. His gut twisted into a knot as his eyes settled on a prone figure on a bed in the room's corner. He hurried back through the concealed passage to his room and into bed, with his heart pounding in his ears and body shivering with dread.

Daniel snapped back to the present. He now wondered why the sight had terrified him so much. Was it because the secret passage behind the panel led from his room to another one he recognized—the one he knew belonged to his sister, Sara? Why did a passageway connect their rooms? Who built it? He recalled he tossed and turned until at least midnight that night, his mind in turmoil.

Daniel never had another opportunity to examine the passageway since the following evening, Patricia and Sara Saviano lost their lives (or so he thought). He wondered if the loose panel was still there. He went to where he recalled it was. His fingers drifted over the wood, and he grinned triumphantly as the board slid free.

* * *

The gauze was saturated with fresh blood, and as Jack squeezed his fingers against the material, he winced in agony. Considering his age and present condition, it amazed him he was even alive. He had returned to the warehouse, and as he considered his choices, he dismissed each one with a modest wave of his free hand.

If he went to the emergency room, chances were excellent that both the staff and the police would identify him. Another choice was to rent a hotel suite on the outskirts of town, where no one would remember him. A less appealing choice for the old mafia boss was his former office building. He heard it had been vacant for the last ten and a half years. "The last time I was there, Janice and I . . ." His mind wandered from the image of his sister-in-law and him discussing arrangements for Patricia's surprise birthday dinner.

Jack's heart ached, not from the bullet fragments inside him but from the memories. He was weeping. He rubbed his face with his bloodied hand. After two minutes of struggling in vain to recover his dignity, forty years of pent-up rage exploded from him. He banged his hand into the wall to his right with such force that the decaying ceiling dropped a cascade of dust particles to the floor beneath him.

So many people had betrayed Jack over four decades. Most paid with their lives, but the individuals he felt most deserved damnation were alive and well. Patricia had lied to him about Sara's condition. Jack realized the truth after having found documents revealing the circumstances surrounding his daughter's birth and the weeks following it. His daughter's health was not nearly as bad as he had been led to believe, and he started to believe there might not be anything wrong with her at all. But that belief later changed, the night after Sara's twelfth birthday, when Jack discovered she had taken his pornographic magazines that depicted nude females. It was then he realized that his daughter was what he despised the most. She might not have had severe hydrocephalus, but there was something that, to him, was potentially even worse for his public image.

From then on, Jack watched Sara's every move so that she could not bring him shame. He cloistered her in her room. Jack set up the concealed space between Daniel and Sara's rooms, devoting many long hours and many days and nights to working in the hidden office so that he could keep tabs on his children's activities. He kept precise notes on things he discovered about his offspring in individual files and hidden compartments in the chamber.

Chapter 20

The Past

Alicia Trevino's soulless eyes reflected the vacuum mortals called death. The coroner's report would show the twenty-one-year-old died in a similar manner to the earlier victims: from a sliced throat. The killer splayed her anatomy out in a fashion like the previous victims. Alicia's mangled corpse stayed in the exact position it fell. Somebody found her body in a low-cost hotel room in the wrong part of town. It appeared the only crime that had been committed was her murder, though. She did not appear to have been raped.

Chapter 21

The Present

Daniel's mind returned to the present. *Why did he come back to this house? What did he hope to accomplish?* Glancing around, he realized his purpose for being there. The messages that led him there evoked a progression of memories he had blocked out for many years—memories like the G-men taking him and his sister away from the bloodbath.

Dan remembered with perfect clarity now: Sara had struggled against him as they fled the gruesome scene of their mother's apparent murder. He was confident that Sara had been trying to refuse to flee with him. Sara did everything in her capacity to separate from his grip. "Let me go, Dan!" she had growled, pushing against his body as she thrust her hands against his chest. "I don't want to go with you!" she objected. "Leave me alone!" She struck him in the chest, making him gulp in agony. Sara did not beg her brother to let her go, she *ordered* it.

As Sara later clung to Daniel in despair that night, he soothed, "You need to stay with me." And tears had welled up in his eyes as he faltered, unsure about where they were going.

Sara had relaxed, and her demeanor softened. "Okay, brother, dear," she conceded, a slow smile touching her mouth. Her tone was so soft that Daniel was not sure he understood what she said next: "It can wait."

Daniel wondered at the time *what* could wait. He understood now. He was in the secret chamber he discovered all those years ago. Little had changed, except for the cobwebs and several inches of thick, stifling dust covering the desk and surrounding the space from many years of nonuse. Folders sat on a shelf, unmoved from the last time Daniel was there. The pages they contained were yellowed and faded. Only the groups on the bottom of the pile were untouched.

Daniel picked up a couple folders from the heap and thumbed through them. These were fascinating readings:

The adolescent displays negative social actions. I have also noted many incidences where the child rejoices in probing the female genitalia. It is natural for a child of the formative years. But there have also been several incidents where the girl has tried to attack her friends and strangers. My point of view is the same as that of several colleagues: the youth should live under continual surveillance by a skilled specialist should her actions continue to escalate.

The document was not dated, and no names were mentioned, but Daniel was sure that Jack Saviano had created it. More details on the adolescent referred to were in the same file. They, too, had identities redacted. Daniel wondered if the allusions were to Sara. Daniel would not have the answer to that question until later.

From the end of the corridor, a pair of eyes studied Daniel in silence. *Dan knows about the secret office. It will not be much longer now until he learns everything. I* knew *we should have destroyed the documents and killed Daniel! I warned Jack!* The onlooker sighed and then uttered a low snicker. *Jack never listened to anybody! If he had, maybe he would be alive right now.* the observer thought.

A noise from behind the person made them spin. They recognized the individual standing there smirking. "See who needed to listen to me?" the figure remarked. The killer smiled as they plunged a blade into the warm flesh of Patricia's belly. "Such a shame you didn't." The killer twisted the dagger around, making the blood surge onto their blue shirt. This was one execution the assassin was sure they would recall and relish for many years to come. Yanking the blade free, they let Patricia's body drop to the floor.

Reaching into an overcoat pocket, the killer pulled out several pieces, placing them around the corpse in a way they considered was like *The Vitruvian Man.* The killer laid each piece, significant to Patricia, around her body. They put the cross Jack gave her on their first anniversary above her skull. When he knew he was to be a parent, he bought her a gold watch. That lay near Patricia's right hand. Her engagement ring and wedding ring, which Jack had engraved, had been missing for three weeks but were now in her left palm. And the crudest of all the arrangements was the Gideon Bible, which lay open on her abdomen and thighs. The killer highlighted a passage on the page. The verse, from Hebrews 10:30, read: *Vengeance is mine; I will repay.*

The killer then removed Patricia's blouse and bra, shredded both with the knife, and tossed them aside. Her body was naked, down to her belly. The killer painstakingly carved various Catholic symbols into the exposed flesh. They sliced her breasts down the middle, cutting the nipples in half. This was the complete degradation in the perpetrator's mind.

The murderer finished the scene off by leaving a white envelope beside Patricia's torso and using Patricia's blood to address it to Daniel. Inside was a handwritten note challenging Daniel: *Find me before I find you.*

Chapter 22

The Past

Leah Hartman walked into her office and jerked the door shut so hard it all but broke on its hinges. She was furious. The plan had gone off without a hitch, except for one detail: the kids fought her. She decided the sensible course of action was to take the kids to the closest shelter until their Aunt Janice could come to collect Sara. Daniel insisted on staying with Sara. Sean had little room to dispute the choice. Leah shrugged out of her dark-purple jacket with a wearied exclamation and rolled up the sleeves of her starched white blouse. An abrupt knock on the door made her jump.

"What?" she called. Her tone was unmistakable—she was irritated. But when she realized who it was, she swallowed hard. What justification for her betrayal might she provide to Jack? Leah had planned for this day. She realized it was inevitable.

"We need to discuss a few issues," Jack announced without introduction as he swung open the door and went into his associate's office. The door slammed shut. Leah stared her son straight in his eyes.

"Such as?" she demanded, crossing the office and taking the leather armchair behind her desk.

"I need to know the truth. Where are my children?" Jack growled. His eyes tightened as he glared at his mother. He slid into the armchair in front of Leah, lifting his overpriced Italian loafers and resting them on the desk. Leaning back, he tucked his palms behind his head. He made himself appear as comfortable as possible to show his mother that despite where she fell in his bloodline, she did not intimidate him. "Where are they?" he repeated, stressing each word. His gaze was intense—so much so, it seemed it could have burned a hole in Leah's eyes. It was a method he perfected over many years and was efficient.

Leah shook her head. "I don't know, Jack, and even if I did, I sure as hell wouldn't enlighten you! Would I?" She laughed. Peering at the stack of documents in front of her, she steepled her fingers as she waited for him to answer her challenge.

The mobster pointed an accusatory finger at her. "Woman," he said, refusing to acknowledge her as his mother, "you are a number one, class A tramp, and I loathe you. I believe you are a harlot, and you slept with not only your first lover but every new guy you met since." Jack scowled as he spoke the insult.

At that, Leah glowered at her offspring. Chest heaving in unmitigated fury, she thrust up from her chair to her highest stature. "You bastard!" she spat out through clenched teeth. Her jaw tensed, and her nostrils flared. "How dare you accuse me of such low action. You are my son, and I demand you regard me with dignity! You and I know, you sick bastard, that your dad was a sympathetic, honorable man who loved you." With those words, she drifted into a regret-filled stroll through a field of dreadful memories. "I wish I could have been there when he died! It wasn't my fault he left on the fishing trip. They never found Charles's body," she recalled, talking more to herself than to Jack.

Jack sneered. "I know what happened to dear old dad, you tramp!" he shrieked and slid his fist into his inner coat pocket. He drew out a Manila envelope and slung it at his mother. "Go on!" he instructed. "Examine the photographs!" He was mocking her now, as though he were playing a game. It was clear he was reveling in the torment.

Leah, to appease both her offspring and her morbid curiosity, opened the envelope. She took out several black-and-white photographs. They were pictures of Charles. The first showed him dressed, bound to a metal chair, and gagged. In the second and third, he was without his jacket and tie, and his shirt was in rags. His chest had several deep gashes in the center, and someone had cut a wide gash in his cheek. The fourth and final photo was the harshest. Charles appeared to be almost beheaded. His exposed throat was a mangled jumble of blood and soft flesh. Dried blood caked around the wounds in his neck, making a bulge under his thyroid. Charles's eyes, once a magnificent and vivid blue, were now cloudy and lifeless. What was left of his skull sank a little to the side. His mouth hung loose, displaying a cavity with several hollow, dry sockets where once perfect teeth had been.

Leah's eyes focused on the last photograph, and she swallowed hard. "Why?" she demanded in a whisper. "What did he do to warrant this? What in the name of all that is holy did you do?"

"Isn't it obvious, Mother dearest? You took what mattered the most to me! You took my children from me, so I have taken the one thing—oh, excuse me, *person*—you adored." Jack wiped his palm across the desk, scattering papers around the office. "You should be God damned lucky it wasn't you instead!" he exploded. Jack resisted the inclination to lean over and slap Leah. Instead, he collapsed and folded his hands, with his fingers held against his dark red lips in thought.

"I suppose I've punished you enough," Jack continued. "What I found fascinating is that Dad seemed invulnerable to the harm I caused him. He only seemed to care what happened to *you*, and he admitted something that shocked me. Can you enlighten me on what he meant by it?" He waited for Leah to acknowledge him with a curious gaze before he concluded. "He said, 'tell your mom I cherished her enough to make sure JEH set her up for life.'" Jack steadied his gaze. "Who is JEH? And why the hell are you trying to double-cross me?"

Leah frowned at her son for a minute, puzzled. "What do you mean, 'why are you trying to double-cross me?'" she challenged. Her face paled as she spoke. Deep down, she realized what he meant. "I haven't sought to double-

114

cross you, Jack," she protested.

Jack scowled at his mom. He produced another envelope from inside his coat pocket. "Dad left this for you, Mother dearest, before he died."

Inside was a note written in Charles's familiar chicken-scrawl handwriting:

I love Leah, so it pains me to write this note. Yet, I have little option. I must double-cross my lover as she has our son in her crosshairs. She is not who she claims to be. I urge you, whoever receives this. Leah Hartman, my loving wife, has been leading a double life. You must locate and deal with her, or she will ruin us all.

Leah met her son's eyes when she stopped reading, and her shoulders sank in sheer embarrassment. "It's true, Jack. I am . . ." A bomb blast from behind the door drowned out her words. It flung mother and son to opposite sides of the office. The last thing Leah saw was the last photograph of her husband. "Charles . . ." she moaned as darkness took her.

Chapter 23

The Past

In school, Daniel always excelled. He was first in his class in high school. For both his junior and senior proms, he had taken Kathy Horton. They went out several times and were even planning on getting married. That was before Kathy's accident. She ended up paralyzed from the waist down, the result of an auto accident. After that, Dan had gone on several more dates with her, but she accused him of going on "pity dates" and ended the relationship, to his dismay.

Kathy still had feelings for Daniel but was nervous it was too late to talk it over. She came to their class reunion, hoping to find him. The girl contemplated telling him how she felt, although she was sure there was no chance of anything meaningful with him. She had heard rumors that Daniel had married and then divorced. Kathy was afraid if the rumors were true, she might have been the reason for the divorce. That was not the case, though. Daniel had married, but the marriage ended because of his wife's reluctance to support a lawman. After the divorce, he moved from Texas and returned to Arizona, which had always been home.

"It's too little, too late!" Kathy mumbled. Staring at the star-filled sky, she didn't notice the man approaching from behind until he spoke, and she jumped, stunned.

"What's that, sweetheart?" the man asked. He paused behind her, and he soothed her as she sat in her wheelchair.

"Jesus Christ!" she squealed, her heart beating in her ears. "You startled the crap out of me!" The hair on her neck prickled as her brain registered the name of the man. "I am sorry, Mr. Saviano!" she apologized. "I didn't notice you standing there." Her face darkened as Daniel's father stepped in front of her and paused. She wanted to be any place but there at that moment. She asked, "Did Dan come to the reunion?" Her eyes had a glimmer of anticipation.

"I'm sorry," Jack responded, shaking his head. "I don't know if my son came or not." A slight grin danced across his dark lips, and he shrugged, his hands jammed into his trousers pockets. Jack dressed for the occasion. He was debonair in his tuxedo, and Kathy inhaled a sigh of admiration. Jack knew his son was there, but he enjoyed taunting her. *God, this is too easy!* he reflected to himself. Stepping closer to Kathy, Jack dropped to one knee in front of her. He put his powerful hands around her throat, and with one deft twist, he jerked her neck until he heard it snap.

Jack pulled Kathy's blanket around her body. He pushed her toward the pool, acting as though they were conversing. Before anyone else showed up, he had made sure the entrance to the pool was unlocked. Opening the gate with a sharp click, Jack thrust the wheelchair through. Whistling, he let go of the brake. He gave it a slight nudge and waited as it advanced toward the side of the pool before plunging into the cold water.

Jack disappeared among the crowd, unseen, as quickly as he had entered. When a group of spectators saw the spray and heard the whir of the chair's electric motor, they noticed the deceased woman floating in the pool. Her stiff body was captured in the churning water and the restraining belts of the wheelchair. One young girl's shriek brought security guards, alumni, and eventually paramedics to the scene. No one could bring the woman back to life.

Chapter 24

The Near Present

I'm dying! Jack thought. From his right, he heard a noise, and he struggled to concentrate on it. It was a kind voice: the sound of an angel and a demon rolled into one soft tone. The voice belonged to *her*. For years, Jack called her by her first name. He refused to acknowledge Leah as the woman who spent nine months with him inside her and then fourteen hours in labor.

Jack groaned as he suddenly felt Leah standing above him. He realized she was peering down at him. With a moan, he tried to sit up but found he couldn't. Mortified, Jack realized that he would have to rely on her to survive. "Why . . . did . . . you . . . shoot me?" Jack managed to get out.

"I didn't. I only grazed you . . . on purpose." Leah's soft voice had an urgency he had never heard from her before, and it scared him. "Come on, dammit! This has to go flawless if you want Daniel to think you are dead!" she hissed. Jack's mother crouched down to drag him over her shoulder.

Jack mumbled an expression implying what she should

119

do with herself but did as she asked anyway, falling limp against her. A few minutes later, with Leah's aid, he was hurled face-first into the garbage bin at the far side of the alleyway. He gasped in agony and uttered a curse. His surroundings muffled the sounds.

"Leah?" Jack demanded a minute after recovering his voice. There was no reply from any direction, except for a lone coyote singing to his mate in the distance. Jack found the noise strange and soothing. Coyotes stayed away from major cities, but they came down into the basins and small towns from the nearby mountains. They hunted at night, staying out of sight during the daylight. An insect he didn't want to identify crept into his pant leg.

"Leah?" he repeated the query after several more minutes of silence. Jack peered over the top of the garbage bin, then fell back and ran a hand across his throbbing chest. Blood was on his shirt. He knew it was his blood, and although the sight of blood never bothered Jack, he wanted to vomit this time. Instead, he passed out.

Chapter 25

The Present

Darkness crept across the city like a beast out of an Anne Rice novel. Daniel had been at home since midnight. He had invited Frank to come to his apartment, having finished at the Hamilton house for the night. Frank arrived with dinner. He also brought a surprise for his friend: a woman.

She was stunning. Her breasts were ample and full. Her hips would make any man's tongue drop to his knees. The young woman stripped free of her clothes and gazed at Daniel, her dark-green eyes shining in the moonlight through the open drapes. Daniel cursed Frank for being so . . . *courteous.*

Frank introduced the woman, who must have been in her early twenties, to Daniel. After tossing him a wink and a knowing grin, Frank slipped from the room.

"Look, um . . ." Dan stammered like a fool. He couldn't remember the woman's name. Daniel shrugged.

"Kris," she supplied, moving toward him. Her hands were gentle as they landed on his shoulders. She caressed Dan's muscles. "Well, my name is Kristina, but my close friends call me Kris." She spoke and then lowered down onto his lap as he was sitting in a leather chair. "Are you okay?"

"I'm fine!" Dan answered, trying to clear his throat. Kris slid down him and almost landed on the floor before he caught her. It was clear she was comfortable with her naked body pressed against him. That was why Dan was finding it so hard to tell her to stop. He put his palms on her shoulders. Clearing his throat several times, he smiled at the woman.

"What is it, Dan?" she asked, frowning at him. She sensed he was nervous, and she stroked his cheek with a hand. "Don't you want me? Don't you want *these*?" She rubbed her palms against her bare breasts, her nipples reacting to the touch of her hands. Kris licked her lips, moving her tongue over them. She knew the effect she was having on Daniel. She had had enough men to know. She might be a prostitute, but she detested the label.

Daniel sighed and released his tight grip on her shoulders. "I think you need to leave, Kris," he said. Dan, a man of the law, could not be caught with a prostitute. But even as he spoke, he let go of his restraints and decided if she did not leave right then, he would take her. God, she was beautiful. "Kris?" Dan called out to her, watching the woman re-dress. Her shoulders were heaving, and it dawned on Daniel that she was crying. Kris looked at him, hope in her eyes.

"Yes?" She replied, heaving a sigh. "What is it?" She sniffled.

Daniel smiled, crossed the room, and held her to him, stroking her hair with his right hand as she wept. "I didn't intend to hurt you, honey," he soothed. "I know you don't understand. Yes, I want you and need you. But I'm a . . ." he drifted off as she raised her eyes to his and shuddered against his body.

"I know, Dan," she responded. "It's ok."

Daniel nodded in understanding. "You know," he said, smiling, "we don't have to do anything but talk." As Kris laid her head on his shoulder, drawing him closer, he realized she did not want to "talk." She wanted *him. God, please don't let me lose control of myself. Shit!*

Kris's hands were on his pants now. She slid Daniel's zipper down, and he inhaled. He was having trouble focusing, and he sucked in a breath. It was no use. His body was responding to the stimuli despite all his efforts to resist her.

"I don't want to talk, Dan," she whispered, but her voice was also thick with a seductive tone. "I . . . want . . . *you!*" she whispered huskily.

Shit, Daniel thought again. Despite everything he did to stay in control, he realized he no longer was. He grabbed Kris, lowering her down onto him, and he showed the girl the proper way to make love. For the first time in years, Daniel smiled. He felt . . . *alive.*

* * *

"**D**an?" Someone was whispering his name through the darkness. A faint glow bathed the far corner in a pale blue light. "Are you awake? Are you okay?"

Dan sighed, squirmed under the sheets, and then sat upright. "I'll be fine," he answered. The phrase was a mantra—one he had adopted over the past several months. It was an automatic response.

Kris straightened up. "Any regrets?" she continued. The woman watched as Dan climbed out of bed and re-dressed. Kris didn't regret her part in it, and she hoped he didn't either. For the first time in her life, she felt comfortable in her skin. With others, they labeled the act as "sex," but with Daniel, it was something more. It was his nervousness or hesitation that turned her on.

Daniel shook his head. "Nope," he replied with a coy wink. He moved over to the bed, bent down, and brushed Kris's lips with his. She responded, her body tensing. Draping her arms around his neck, she pulled him down, deepening the kiss. With a soft moan, he drew back. "I need—" he began, but he stopped short as the door swung open and Frank thrust his head in.

"Dan!" Frank cried out. His eyes were wide, his blond hair was tousled, and his brown shirt and pants appeared rumpled as though he dressed in a hurry. He was oblivious to the pair standing in the middle of the room half-naked. "We have a 901H at the Hamilton house. You should see this." A 901H, Dan knew, was police code for a "dead body." He was already wearing clothes by the time Frank returned to the hallway.

Daniel glanced at Kris and shrugged as he followed Frank out the door, motioning for her to stay put. Twenty minutes later, they were inside Dan's former home again. He practically flew through the front door. When he came around the corner at the end of the hallway and saw the body, Daniel almost fainted. *It was his mother!*

Patricia's lifeless eyes stared up at Dan. "How could you let this happen?" they demanded. Daniel rubbed the side of his face with a hand, forcing back a sob. Biting his bottom lip so hard he drew blood, he turned and made his way back to the bedroom. Daniel longed to hold her, hear her voice, and smell the sweet, scented lilac perfumed soap she used. There was so much Dan had wanted to learn from her about what had become of their family. *Where had she been all these years? What had she been doing? Why did she cheat on his dad? How many men had she had affairs with?*

"Where the hell is the coroner?" Dan asked someone who had walked past the room. He grabbed the man's arm, swinging him around to stare him in the face. "Bring me a God damned sheet or something to cover . . ." He stopped to keep from saying, "the body." The other man shrank a little, and for a minute, Dan assumed he would cry. Instead, he scowled, turned on his heel, and marched off to find a sheet as instructed.

Dan opened his mouth to call after him but stopped as the energy to do so left him. He felt his knees buckle, and he felt dizzy. Before he realized what was happening, his feet slid out from under him. He hit the floor with a thud.

To Dan's shock, as he came to, Kris was standing over him, her hand extended toward him. "Hey. I wanted to make sure you are okay, so I came after you," she murmured, grasping his hand in hers. Squatting beside him, Kris smiled. Her eyes drifted to the body, which was now covered. "Who is it?" she asked Daniel. "Someone said she was your mom. Is that true?"

Dan closed his eyes again, considering the answer before he gave it. "Yes," he whispered, choking on the word. A sudden wave of nausea washed over him, and he shifted, letting his vomit spill onto the carpet beside him. He alerted someone nearby before he did it. Dan wiped his mouth with his handkerchief. He contemplated lying to Kris, but he promised himself the lies would end. He forced a smile. "So, um . . . how did you end up here?" Dan was asking Kris how she knew to find him there. He hadn't told her the address.

Kris gazed at Dan for a long while before she spoke. When she responded, her tone took on at least thirty more years. She sounded twice her age. "My dad was, if you can believe it, an undercover operative. Mom and my sister, Kathy, soon tired of him and his constant 'missions.'" She drew a nervous breath and then went on with the story. "She took us away one night, and we never looked back. I never learned what happened to dad, but I guess I take on after him. Well, there's that, and . . . I simply asked Frank," she said with smile.

"Your sister's name was *Kathy*?" Dan asked, his ears perking at the name. At Kris's quizzical frown, he revealed, "I knew someone named Kathy a long time ago." He asked, "How old is she, if you don't mind me asking?"

He wondered whether her sister was the same Kathy he had fallen in love with.

Kris said nothing for a few minutes. "She would have been forty-three years old next Saturday." She twisted away so he could not see her face. Kris was happy that Kathy was dead. She *hated* the woman, although there was no logical reason.

The significance of the woman's response was not lost on Daniel. *Would have been?* the words echoed in his mind.

Kris nodded. "Yes, honey. Someone murdered Kathy at her twenty-five-year reunion. She had been so excited about seeing her former classmates. And she had hoped to run into her high school boyfriend there." Passing a nervous hand across her face, Kris turned toward Dan once again.

Dan groaned and clambered to his feet. He wanted to run away. But despite his best efforts, Dan found he could not make his feet obey his brain. Dan braced against the wall once more. He had somehow missed Kathy's file during his review of unsolved murder cases and had not, in fact, attended the reunion himself. So, he had no knowledge of Kathy's murder. "My dad . . ." he gasped, battling to breathe and speaking more to himself than to Kris. "It had to have been Jack." Surely, Jack was the murderer.

Daniel shut his eyes as he sought to ignore the image of his mother's body. The coroner would be there in an hour. Kris's words echoed in his ears, and he worked to control his temper. "You mentioned," he said at last, "that someone murdered Kathy. How did it happen?"

Kris stared at Daniel, her eyes widening in surprise. This question was the last one she expected him to ask. "They say she drowned after having her neck broken." The girl turned and stared out the window into the darkness. With a sob, she said, "The police claim they have no leads, but I know Jack Saviano is the guilty party." She raised her palm to ward off the obvious question and tossed her head to one side, finishing, "I just know. Don't ask me how."

Daniel watched the woman for what seemed an eternity. He wrung his hands, then stood and touched Kris's shoulder with a palm. "What makes you suspect Jack?" he asked with a frown. His eyes searched hers for a moment, as though seeking the answer.

Kris sighed, her shoulders dropped, and she felt faint. "Because he barely even knew her, but he was at the funeral, Dan." She rested her head against his shoulder, inhaling his cologne. "He thought I didn't recognize him, but I did. Everyone in the community knows Jack Saviano." Kris hoped to make love to Daniel again someday but knew that now, with his mother dead and the revelation that his father was a murderer, he had too much to deal with.

Chapter 26

The Past

Keith Horton slid from the driver's seat of his car and stretched. He heard several bones in his back pop, and he groaned. Keith was getting too damn old for this and knew it. *He had a job to do, and, by God, Keith would do it . . . Or die trying.* Even for a man of his advanced age, Keith walked to the red-brick building where he and Jack had agreed to meet with some difficulty. *I am doing this for them*, he assured himself, feeling the weight of the world on his shoulders.

"About time you showed up, you old sea dog!" a voice called out, startling Keith out of his stupor. "I've been waiting here for a half-hour, old man."

Keith planted himself in a leather chair and stretched. He glanced up and forced a smile. "Well, Jack, you know how bad traffic can sometimes be." Passing a hand through his sandy-brown hair, he added, "And I got a ticket from one of our finest." He reached into his pocket and withdrew the slip of paper that claimed the police cited him. It was a fake, given to him by a source in the department. He needed to keep the ruse going. He knew it would help bring down the monster who destroyed so many lives.

Jack smiled at Keith, taking the ticket from the other man's outstretched hand without hesitation. He gave the paper nothing more than a cursory glance and handed it back to him. Shrugging, Jack sat in the empty chair across the desk from Keith. "It is no matter, my friend," he said. Leaning back, Jack steepled his fingers and touched them to his lips in thought—a well-practiced move that meant he was ready for the kill. Keith was Jack's one connection between his world and the world he had created for the public eye and intended to keep intact. "I'm sure you know why I called you here," Jack added, a slow smile creeping across his face.

Keith felt his heart hammering in his ears, and he let out a shaky breath, trying to calm himself. They had warned him what could happen. For the moment, he stayed still. The next move would be up to Jack. Keith had always been the consummate chess player; Jack was the pawn in this continuing game.

Jack arched an eyebrow, waiting for a reply. Getting none, he shrugged. "Your wife is beautiful, Keith, old chap. It would be a pity to see her face mangled beyond recognition, don't you think?"

Keith blanched at the implication. Somehow Jack had discovered the truth. He dropped the mask. "You wouldn't dare!" he whispered, closing his eyes, trying to keep from losing his temper. Keith promised himself he wouldn't let Jack gain any further control over him or his family. Jack was trying to do that. He manipulated Keith even now, and Keith felt powerless to stop it from happening.

Keith did not beg Jack not to do anything to his wife or daughters; it was futile. Instead, Keith tried a fresh approach. "I'll do whatever you want, Jack. I won't waste my time and energy or yours begging you to spare my family. I know it won't do them or me any good." He grinned as an idea came to him. "I would rather dispose of them myself." Keith made his tone sound as though he were flippant about what happened to his family.

Jack smiled. "Are you prepared to *execute* them, my friend? It's the only way the plan will progress. You will kill them all." He hesitated. Showing his polished teeth, he resembled a shark in the bright lights of the room. He finished, "Because if you don't, Keith . . ." Jack produced a gun from inside his jacket. He slid it across the table. "I will tell your buddy down at the agency you killed yourself." Jack winked, and Keith paled as he recognized the photograph on the table as his image. The man standing beside Keith in the photograph was someone recognizable. It was his partner, Thomas Anderson. "You try to double-cross me again, old bean, and I swear I will make your life a living hell. Do I make myself clear, Keith?"

Keith stared at the photograph in complete silence for several minutes. He took the picture, crumpling it up in his palm, snarling, "Go to hell, you asshole."

Jack shrugged, his grin broadening. "Oh, believe me, old man, I've been there already. I quite enjoyed the atmosphere. They told me I'd be seeing *you* there." He clucked his tongue and slid his hand into his jacket. After a second, he removed his hand and rose to his feet. Keith saw the stiletto in Jack's hand seconds too late to react, and a moment later, Jack sliced his throat clean. Jack laughed as he grabbed the crumpled photo and, with a rage he barely concealed, stuffed the photograph into the gaping wound. Turning to a hidden figure, he roared, "Get this jackass out of my sight!"

The person and two of Jack's bodyguards kneeled to slide the body into a body bag. One of them asked, "How do you want us to dispose of the corpse?"

Jack smiled at the new arrivals. "Why don't you bring him home to his family?" After a pause, he added, amused, "Don't forget to gift-wrap the body, too."

Leah glanced up at her son and nodded. She regretted this part of her job, but she expected it. It was unavoidable. This would be one of many deaths at the hand of a monster. She wished she could have saved Keith. She had grown fond of him over the previous months. He was her informant—her contact with the outside world. Leah knew his wife and kids could escape with her help.

Chapter 27

The Present

Leah awoke from the nightmare screaming. Sweat streamed from every pore in her body. She vowed to stop the maniac her son turned into, and Keith's murder had been the breaking point. There would be no more deaths by either her hand or her son's.

She sat up on the bed, inspecting the surrounding room, unable to see clearly. Daniel had called her a few hours earlier to inform her about Patricia's death. There wasn't a need to elaborate; she already knew who was responsible. Leah wondered why she hadn't realized Patricia wasn't at the hotel. She chalked it up to being too exhausted to notice.

Sitting on the corner of the bed, Leah realized she still wore the same clothes from the previous day. She had come into the room, lay down on the bed, and immediately fallen asleep. Considering all that happened, it amazed her she could sleep. The memories from all those years ago still haunted her, and she shuddered, fighting to draw an even breath.

With shaking hands, Leah stood. She crossed the

room and sat by the open laptop on the desk. She woke it from sleep mode and reviewed her email. Sighing, she realized it was mostly spam. This was thankless work. It was for the greater good, though. Soon enough, the ones who helped organized Jack's evil enterprise would be where they belonged, either dead or behind bars. Leah could move on and resume her normal life.

What was "normal," though? It had been so long since Leah could lead a "normal" life. She forgot what it meant to get up in the morning, kiss the husband she loved, dress, and go to a semi-normal job with reasonable pay and regular work hours. Leah felt a pang of remorse as she considered Charles and how he died all those years ago. Shutting out the images, she shifted her attention back to the computer. Creating a new message, she typed a brief note and sent it, telling her superiors what had happened over the past several days. "I'm awaiting further instructions." She finished the email, adding that her contact should call her on her cell phone soon, and then she shut the laptop off. It was only a matter of time until it would all be over.

Leah had learned to wait over the last forty-odd years. "I can wait a few more hours," she confirmed to herself. She crossed the room to the kitchenette and opened the refrigerator. Taking a can of Pepsi, she shut the door, staring out the window into the morning sky. The weather report called for at least another six inches of snow. With a grimace, Leah walked to the television and turned it on. Opening the can, she took a long drink but choked as she caught sight of the news bulletin.

On the screen was a black-and-white photograph of Thomas Anderson. He had been Charles and Leah's primary contact with the FBI. Thomas was the last one to see Charles alive before Charles's disastrous meeting with Jack. "Early this morning, the body of former FBI agent Thomas Anderson was identified after going missing thirty-five years ago. He left behind his wife, Maria, and a daughter, Marcia. His partner, Keith Horton, also vanished around the same time. Police speculated that Anderson might have been responsible for Horton's disappearance or murder."

Leah scowled at the television, turning it off in exasperation. She muttered a few swear words and then reached for her cell phone. Punching in a number, she hit "Call." "I saw the news about Anderson," she said when the person on the other end answered. "What are we supposed to do?" She hesitated, listened to the response, and said, "No. Do you hear me? No more! I am done with all of it! I want out!" She ended the call and sent the phone hurling across the room. She drank the remaining soda and flung the can into the nearby wastebasket in disgust. Hot tears burned her cheeks as they burst from her eyes. With those last words, she chose her destiny.

* * *

The dreams continued to haunt the killer. They woke up shouting from the visions that still lingered. For a second, the killer believed blood covered their hands. But it was

135

actually the reflecting red neon "Vacancy" signs outside the hotel room. There was more detail now. The memories were invading the killer's mind . . .

"What do you mean it's over for us, Jeannie, honey? You promised me you would help me get through this!" A sudden burst of tears stung the killer's eyes and cheeks.

Jeannie grasped the arms of the bamboo chair, and her knuckles turned white. She thought they would break under pressure. Her voice shook, and her bottom lip quivered. Jeannie explained: "I mean, I went back to John. I've been living a lie by being with you. I have lied to you, him, and even myself. Now, do not look at me that way! You know what I'm saying is the truth! Think about it for a while. Admit . . ."

"Shut up! It is a horrible lie. You're a liar! Remember what you came here for? I didn't invite you! I thought I told you never to come back! You have ten minutes to leave. Then I will be back. If you are still here, lover boy John will have something to think about!"

Jeannie turned and walked to the far end of the house, but she never made it out alive. They would never find Jeannie Macon's body.

Snapping back to reality, the killer thrust upward and stood. *When will the dreams end?* they wondered, heaving a disgusted sigh. The hallucination of blood disappeared, but the shaking continued. *God, I need a drink!* Crossing the room, the killer went to the minibar and grabbed whatever they could find. Not caring they did not have glasses or cups handy, the killer pulled the cork free and drank straight from the bottle. The liquid was warm and calmed the murderer's unsteady hands.

"Do you think it's that easy to forget me?" The sudden question startled the killer from their trance. They almost dropped the bottle in shock. "You must think you acted rationally! Newsflash, honey: you didn't! I won't let you get away with this!"

"What the hell?" The killer said, whirling and looking around. But no one else was there. They swore someone spoke. With a dismissive shrug, they put the cork in the bottle and returned it to the minibar.

A soft chuckle came from the far corner of the room. The killer gasped as a physical body took shape in front of her. "I told you, didn't I, that you wouldn't be able to forget me! Oh, don't look so surprised to see me. I am not here. I am yet another part of your delusion that you are a rational creature. Call me your conscience, Pinocchio!"

"Get out! Leave me the hell alone! I killed you once, Jeannie . . . I don't want to have to . . ." The killer let the rest of the sentence go instead of finishing with "do it again." Collapsing from dizziness, pain medication, and nausea, unconsciousness took the killer away for the next several hours. The killer was going mad and knew it. *It was all their fault, both of them—the men I thought were my father and brother*, they thought. The only way for the killer to keep their sanity, they vowed, was to destroy them both, just like they had tried to destroy *her*.

Chapter 28

The Past

The murderer waited, their hands clasped around the small stiletto, for the victim to scream and beg for her life. Unlike the others, Sheryl Watkins was not caught by surprise. Sheryl expected this turn of events because she said, "Don't stand there, my love. You and I both know you want to kill me."

The killer and victim regarded each other for a few seconds until the knife slipped from the killer's hand, clattering against the linoleum floor. "Yes." It was a soft reply. And this time, the killer regretted it. "I do." Sighing, they seized the knife, still caked with blood from the earlier murders. "Do you understand why?"

Sheryl shrugged, spreading her arms out wide. "You are doing it for me. I am a whore in your eyes. You want me to die and pay for my sins. This is your way of making me atone." She hesitated. "You also see it as a chance to redeem me: blood for blood and all that shit." Sheryl laughed, glancing up at the murderer. "What's stopping you? Do it!" The auburn-haired woman reached upward and wrenched the knife from the killer's hand. "Why are

138

you waiting? Kill me already! Take my life!"

For a moment, the killer watched Sheryl with confusion. They saw something that made them question everything they believed. "Why do you want to die?" the killer asked, surprised by Sheryl's words.

"I told you: blood for blood. You said that last night you lost something. I want to give it back." Sheryl shrugged. "I want you to murder me. You need to kill me." Sheryl caressed the hilt of the knife, a seductive smile playing across her face. "Do it. Please!"

A sigh escaped the murderer's lips. *God, but Sheryl is right. She . . . is . . . right!* Rather than plunging the knife into the woman's flesh, the killer snatched the weapon away and dropped it to the floor. They took Sheryl's hand in theirs. "I am tired—exhausted. I want you. This is what I've needed for so long. I thought you were like the others. I hoped you were!" The killer smiled. "But you aren't, are you?" Running their hand through Sheryl's long auburn hair, they pulled her to them and let their reservations go free. The murderer knew the potential prey would escape a brutal death by their hands.

Chapter 29

The Present

Leah Hartman approached the empty warehouse that had contained the head offices of the Saviano criminal enterprise. She was cautious of returning there, scared of what she might find. It had been many years since she had been there last. Why she returned now, not even she knew. Leah knew returning would only complicate things. Jack had ordered her to do so many horrible deeds over the past four decades. Despite being an FBI agent, she was helpless to prevent any of them or it would have blown her cover.

Jack didn't care who he hurt or how. For him, it was about influence and power. Leah realized that long ago when Jack revealed what he had done to her husband—his father, Charles. Leah shuddered, both against the cold and the mental imagery she conjured of that day. Unlike the other buildings around the area, this building complex had not been rebuilt. Leah wanted it that way so that Jack would have to live with the memory of what nearly killed them all.

Pulling her green overcoat tighter around her, Leah

stared up at the remaining section of the building, which had been Jack's personal office. Years of inclement weather and vagrants living there changed the once-solid structure into near-rubble. The mysterious bomb that had gone off had not helped, either.

Leah had always wondered what happened but assumed that Jack had tried to destroy his own building. But now, years later, she questioned if he had really been the one responsible. She placed a leather-gloved palm against the wall, closing her eyes. She wondered if there was anything to the ability to "see" the past—there was an opinion that most parents develop a telepathic bond with their children. But after a moment standing there with her palm against the wall, Leah lowered her hand and shrugged. *There was nothing to the theory*, she decided. She experienced nothing. She did not "see" anything that happened she did not already know.

It surprised Leah when a voice broke through her reverie. She startled and almost screamed but calmed herself. "I thought I might find you here, old woman. Decades go by, and you still believe you can figure out what happened to your 'loving' husband."

Leah caught her breath and eyed the man standing there. He stuffed his hands into his pants pockets and looked no worse or better since she saw him the previous night. "I still wonder about that night," she said, drawing in a long, calculated breath. She wanted to intimidate him, but he wasn't a fool. "About what happened to Jack, and what made the bomb detonate? Was it *you*?" she asked, narrowing her eyes at him. The man standing there wasn't a murderer, and they both knew it. Still, she felt the question was one she needed to ask.

The man shrugged as he considered his answer. It wasn't an admission of guilt or denial. "There's more going on here than you know, I'm afraid. The mysterious bombing all those years ago was a flawed interpretation of instruction by someone within the agency who thought they were handling things." He stared at Leah for a long, silent moment. He exhaled. "Don't waste your time trying to figure out what happened. Accept it and go forward," he advised, turning to leave.

Leah stared at his receding form and then called out: "Why did you come back after all these years? What did you think you could do now?" Arching an eyebrow, she crossed her arms over her chest, waiting for him to speak. She was curious to know what he thought, what he felt. She added, "Almost everyone is dead. What difference does it make?"

"It's time, Leah," he responded. The man was used to talking in riddles; it had gotten him far in his many occupations through the years. The figure lowered his eyes to the ground and then met her gaze, asking, "Would you mind if I gave you a word of advice? For God's sake, don't be another one." Leah understood the warning: don't be another victim. "You destroyed everything by coming here and opening the door to Daniel's memories. You should have let *us* handle it."

Leah sighed and reached out her hand toward the

man. "You know, I couldn't let it go. It wouldn't take long before Daniel remembered what happened and before he asked questions." She bit her lip and added, "And I remember how your team handled things that night. 'Danny will not remember the truth. Don't worry, he'll forget everything Jack tried to do to us,' you told me. God, Charles, what the hell was I supposed to be doing when he saw Jack shoot Patricia? What was I supposed to tell him? *Oh no, Danny, it was just a dream. Go back to sleep?*"

Charles moved his lips to reply, threw up his hands in disgust, and then responded mockingly, "I suppose you have all the answers he needs? Did you know someone tried to cut his brake lines last night?" At Leah's look of surprise, he added, "Oh, you needn't worry, I assure you. I called in a few favors and had them repaired while he was asleep. It comes in handy to know people, don't you think?" A mirthless grin and a chuckle followed. And then Charles sobered. The man shrugged. They were both tired, he realized. Too tired to continue the old argument.

Once, many years ago, Charles had considered filing for a divorce, but the more he worked with Leah, he discovered it would be impossible to ask for a transfer to another department. They'd wed in secret because it was against the bureau's rules to be married to a partner.

Leah nodded. She wanted nothing to happen to her grandson, so she was thankful for this man's prompt intervention. "You better go," she said as she squeezed his hand.

143

Charles returned the gesture, a half-smile playing on his lips. "I mean it. You need to watch your back. I will not be around forever, you know." He kissed her and drew back. "Don't disappoint me, please. I have had faith in you and your abilities over the years." He walked away. His figure shuddered against the chilly night air as he pulled his dark-blue overcoat tighter. The temperature had dropped at least five degrees in the last half an hour. It would be a cold evening. They would have another six inches of snowfall by midmorning, according to the weather report.

As Charles turned to depart, Leah whispered, "I wish Jack hadn't murdered your twin, Charles." She willed him to turn around, to look her in the eye, and tell her everything would work out for the best. Leah wanted to hear the words. But she knew nothing would be all right. Fate had been brutal to her over the decades. Time had affected her.

Charles did not reply, only stiffened. For a moment, he said nothing, and then he turned once again to face his wife. *God, I love her so much. If I allow this to continue, it may kill her*, he thought. There was so much bloodshed throughout the years, some by his hand and some by his son's. Charles knew it would be only a matter of time before it all ended. He had already risked far too much by following Leah. Still, he knew he had no other choice and would continue to watch out for his spouse and grandson. But not even he could predict what the next several hours would bring. If—and that was a big "if"—he had been able to, then there wouldn't have been two more deaths.

Charles turned toward his wife and gently put his hand on her cheek. He wanted so much to hold her, to kiss her, to take her so far away from all this. But he knew it would be useless. Time had taken its toll on them both. He knew that the longer he stayed, the harder it would be to let her do what she needed to do. Charles had taken a major risk by following and meeting her. If anyone knew he came, it would be disastrous.

* * *

Daniel stood in the back of the room, his hands thrust deep into his pants pockets. He wore a simple brown suit. The necktie felt like it was suffocating him, and he struggled to straighten it, almost choking as it tightened around his neck. People drifted around the mortuary, chatting among themselves. Sometimes people would glance his way and then continue to murmur in hushed tones as if they thought he couldn't hear them, even though he could. Daniel ignored everything he heard people saying anyway.

He sighed and accepted the cup of water someone offered, drinking it down in several long gulps. Despite being exhausted, he had not slept for the past couple of nights. His colleagues had done their job with his mother's corpse. There was no reason for an autopsy. Daniel turned down the recommendation. He knew, without a doubt, what killed her. It was not "what" but "who" that mattered now. Is it possible Jack had survived? Daniel thumbed the envelope he had tucked away in his jacket—

the envelope he had discovered on his mother's body—and shook his head. Although she had been unfaithful to Jack, his mother was still a human being. Jack had no right to kill her.

Daniel opened his eyes as he heard a familiar voice. "If you will all find your seats, please, we can start the service." It was Eli Fredericks, the mortuary director. Daniel sat in the nearest chair and crossed his legs. He chose a closed casket. He had wondered how many people would show up for the memorial and was surprised to see the room packed. The overflow ran into the adjoining room. He knew his mother affected many lives but was still surprised.

Daniel listened as Eli and others droned on about how good a person his mother was. She was active in church as a young woman, which carried over into adulthood, they claimed. Daniel almost laughed aloud at those comments. He never once recollected her attending any church. Considering Daniel had walked in on her and her lover, in his eyes, Patricia had never been God-fearing anyway.

Daniel had made no progress—at least none he could admit to his colleagues—in solving his mother's murder. He glanced around the room and realized his sister was nowhere in sight. That was unusual because he remembered she favored her mother more than she did Jack. Daniel remembered the notes his father had written about his sister—the ones he had found in the secret passageway. They painted her as a disturbed adolescent. Daniel's memory of his sister differed from that depiction.

For Daniel, his sister had been a beautiful and loving, albeit timid, young woman. Her teenage years were filled with constant affection from their mother and father—he supposed because they knew she would not outlive them. But the documents Daniel had seen in the secret room painted a different picture of his younger sibling. It made sense that Patricia did not know about her daughter's secret life and desires, considering Jack had mostly locked Sara away. Other than for school, the night they thought their mother had died was one of the only times in Sara's entire childhood she had been outside the house.

Dan recalled a memory from when they were children. Jack and Patricia had argued about his sister. This memory upset him, considering he was outside their bedroom door when the argument occurred . . .

"She needs structure in her life, Jack. I do not want her to feel like she needs to stay here for the rest of her life. She must learn and grow. I don't like her trapped here in this house day in and day out. I know it would give us all a break."

Jack grunted as he lifted his shoulders upward in a half shrug. "You want our daughter to be a pariah? You don't know what kids are like now. It is different today than when we were kids, Patti."

Patricia looked up, dropped the necklace she held in her hand into the wooden jewelry box, and smirked. "Don't you dare," she said through clenched teeth, "tell me that our daughter is not any of that. Don't talk me into

147

leaving her secluded in her bedroom like a Catholic nun." She scowled, grabbing her makeup sitting on the table in front of her. Patricia did not care for the "womanly" look. But considering she and Jack were going out to dinner with family and friends, she wanted to look her best. It was all about appearances for Jack Saviano.

Jack opened the closet door and peered inside at the business suits that hung in the closet. He ran his fingers over a dark gray suit and then shook his head, deciding whether to wear it. Opting instead for the dark blue suit next to it, he spread the suit out on the bed. "I am saying nothing of the sort, my darling," he whispered as he turned toward the bathroom. He was standing there topless, and he smiled at Patricia's reflection in the vanity mirror. "I am telling you we should at least consider the alternative. What life will Sara have if she may mingle with children who don't know how to handle someone who is . . . ?" He drifted off, searching for words to describe his progeny.

Patricia scowled at him in the mirror, sickened by his reflection. Jack had been a handsome man with bright eyes and wavy hair that had turned the heads of everyone who crossed his path. Now, over forty years after she had fallen in love with him, Jack had aged, his face wrinkled and worn from time, and his once-full red lips were now pale and drawn into a carefully lined grimace. He never smiled or laughed these days. Patti wanted more than a friendly pat on the arm or a kiss on the cheek. She craved passion. But those days were long gone. Now it was a marriage of convenience.

"Sara can think and is a very loving, alert human be-ing!" Patricia assured Jack. "She can live like a typical American teenager who may go to school and have friends. She should fall in love like anyone else her age. She should be free to bond with whoever she chooses." Patricia was breathing harder as she spoke. Her voice raised several octaves. "Even if it is another girl, as she seems to prefer," she added.

Jack grabbed a folded towel from the edge of the bed. He had the urge to knot it around his wife's neck and choke the life from her. It would solve all his problems in an instant, he thought, and he rejoiced in the thought of committing another murder. He wanted to feel the life slip from his wife's body and the arousal it brought as she struggled against him. After a second, he collected him-self, turned to the bathroom door, and let out the breath he held in a whoosh of air. There would be more chances, Jack supposed. It was only a matter of time. Besides, he was already thinking of the beautiful, long-legged, blonde-haired server at the restaurant. Jack whistled to himself as he went to take his shower. He left Patricia alone to fume in silence.

Daniel shuddered at the memory and let out a shaky breath. He realized he was crying. Hot tears ran down his cheeks, and he reached for his handkerchief to dab at them. During the closing prayer, Daniel glanced up at Aunt Janice, who had been sitting next to Leah. The women were subdued the whole time. Now, he noticed,

149

they clung together in despair. The scene was surreal to Daniel; he knew the two women had not spoken in years. Janice had been bitter toward Jack and Patti because she thought Sara had been "thrown into her life."

Leah and Janice rose together from their seats and hurried for the exit. Daniel wanted to stop them; he wanted to explain what had happened to Jack. He knew in time that Leah would tell her sister-in-law the truth, though, so he let the pair go with a brief acknowledgment. Leah returned to the room a few minutes later. The look on her face spoke volumes for Daniel, but he asked the obvious question anyway: "Why didn't you go to the hotel with her?"

Leah put her arm on her grandson's shoulder, leaned in, and whispered, "I know it isn't the time or place, but we need to talk." Leah straightened up and took Daniel by the arm, leading him toward the exit and then toward her car. Leah glanced around the parking lot, pulled her coat tighter around her body, and instructed Daniel, "Get in." As they climbed into the car, she felt uneasy, as if she sensed someone watching them. Leah shrugged off the paranoia and locked her seat belt in place.

When the car pulled from the parking lot, a dark figure stepped into the light. Then, they slipped back into the shadows, afraid someone would see them. The figure wasn't quite ready to confront Daniel yet. "Only a matter of time," the person whispered, "and it will be finished. I have waited a lifetime, Danny. I can wait a little longer to kill you," they said, repeating their earlier vow. Smiling, the killer touched the bloodstained stiletto in their jacket pocket. After Leah's car had disappeared into the darkness, the figure turned and walked away.

Chapter 30

The Past

The killer stared down at the body before them. Passing the dagger from one hand to the other, they sighed. The woman before this one died even more ruthlessly than the earlier four. The killer shredded her breasts and yanked hair from her scalp by the handfuls, leaving tiny red dots scattered across the flesh. The lips were sewn with an expert's stitch. The woman only saw her attacker for less than five minutes before her eyes were sewn shut, too. Her neck was bruised as if someone had tried to strangle her, but the killer had slashed her throat instead. These gruesome facts were revealed in recent newspaper issues, and the city was both terrified and outraged. The victim's daughter swore vengeance against her mother's killer.

The new, most recent, victim worked for a law firm on the far side of town, and this was the most gruesome murder yet. There was a rumor one of the firm's clients was none other than Jack Saviano. The city brought Jack up against the Grand Jury for at least four counts of aggravated assault against a police officer, attempted bribery of a government official, and various other crimes. Saviano denied all claims and hired not one but three separate lawyers from different firms. The killer turned the blade over several times in their gloved hand and shook their head, trying to push the cobweb forming inside away.

The killer realized there was no logical reason for these killings except the compulsion to commit them. And the murderer found that with each drop of blood spilled, they were sinking deeper into the regret that always followed the act. Submission, once achieved, was gratifying and electrifying for them. During the act of stabbing and cutting the victims, the killer experienced something akin to an orgasm. It wasn't sexual in the usual sense of the word; it was later, once a woman's life force drained. Only then did the act give the killer a familiar sense of release. But then . . . regret.

What nature of monster would enjoy the thrill of not only the chase and capture but the kill as well? The killer thought back through their life as they wiped the bloodied knife against their dark slacks and held their breath as memories flooded their brain . . .

"Our child needs the chance to grow, to survive. Honey, I know we agreed she could not handle the cruelties of life she has dealt with. But circumstances have changed." Their mother spoke in a whisper, and the child strained to hear her soft voice against the falling rain on the bedroom window.

"The cruelties of life?" their father repeated, his voice rising as he spoke. "Are you mad, woman? There is no crueler fate than someone's child subjugated to an

outsider's propaganda of what life is supposed to be. My God." He threw up his hands in disgust. He turned, for the first time aware someone else was hearing his words. "Leave it alone, my darling. Our child will live. Oh yes, have no worries about that. But it will be as I see fit. Stand in my way, and you will suffer." The man frowned, speaking to both his wife and the unseen person listening.

At the man's threatening words, the child drew back against the wall. She worked her way back to her room, opening the door. Despite what everyone thought they knew about the child being incapable of everyday movement, she flopped down on her bed with ease. The ten-year-old made a vow at that moment: no one would rule her or tell her what to do ever again. God help anyone that tried. If they did, they would die.

Snapping back to reality, the killer sighed. They had perfected the vow. And they had learned not to be careless with the kill, which made it harder for law enforcement to identify them or the victims. The first two were sloppy killings; the killer left markers of every kind on the bodies. But the third and fourth were done neater. Practice, as they say, makes perfect. The last victims would be the ones to stand out to the authorities and to the individual who the killer wanted to know they were responsible. After every kill, they experienced a feeling akin to sexual euphoria. They couldn't accept it as an orgasm, but it came close.

"So, tell me," the killer said now, as though the new victim were still alive, "was dying worth your betrayal?

Did you feel as aroused as me as my blade sliced open your chest and your blood flowed free of its captive vessel? Did the final twitches of your body as you breathed out your last breath give you a frenzy of emotion and physical ecstasy?" The killer twirled the knife in their gloved hands and smiled, rocking back and forth on their heels. Chuckling, eyelids half-closed, they plunged the knife into the woman's chest again and then flung back, giving up the soul of the victim before them.

Chapter 31

The Present

Daniel stared into the vastness of the night sky. He felt he had aged at least a hundred years over the past several days. Everything happened quickly. He wasn't even sure what day it was. He and Leah had driven, in total silence, to the property where Jack had run his then-successful investment business. Dan stared at the rubble that remained of the building.

"Your dad was proud of you, Dan." Leah's voice seemed to come from nowhere, and Dan jumped, startled. A foot of snow still covered the surrounding ground. It had been a long time since it last snowed this much in Arizona. Even now, snowflakes were cascading down to the ground. Leah was standing behind him, her hands thrust into her deep overcoat pockets. She shivered, and her teeth chattered as she talked.

Daniel grunted, raising his head to the stars. "Why can't I believe that?" he asked, voicing his thoughts. His eyes flashed in the brightness of the single lamppost. He touched the remnants of the wall that stayed standing. With a half-smile, he glanced at Leah, waiting for her to answer the question.

"I know it's hard to believe," she replied, "but it's true. You want to know why I brought you here?" Leah reached into her pocket and removed a locket from her jacket. "I am trying to get you to remember everything, and here's one more memory. Does this look familiar to you?" she inquired, narrowing her eyes at him. She stared hard into his eyes, gauging his response. The necklace was made of pure gold. It was heart-shaped and unfamiliar to Daniel. Leah had opened the locket as she spoke. One faded photograph was inside. She dropped it in his outstretched palm, continuing to hold his gaze.

"Should it?" Daniel asked, his eyebrows furrowing into a deep frown. As he stared at the photograph, his head spun, and he became dizzy. He suddenly recognized the small child. Dan now remembered the locket belonged to Patricia. He refused to say the name of the person in the photograph, though. The name invoked a dozen memories, some good, some horrifying. Still, Daniel knew Leah was waiting for an answer. "Is he alive?" Daniel asked, his voice breaking at Leah's solemn nod and smile. "Where's my brother? Where is Jared?" The tears for the boy missing for the better part of Daniel and Sara's lives finally began to fall.

* * *

Jared Saviano stared across the vast ocean and trembled. He had traveled over a thousand miles in less than four days. It was futile to confront his past, but he felt he had to try. He almost went mental from the horrific scene playing in his mind since that fateful night years earlier. Jared did not come on this cruise for pleasure but instead for business. There was a rumor that his father, Jack Saviano, was alive and on board. The *boy* in him was terrified to face the man who had seemed so threatening during his childhood. But the *man* in him needed to do so. There had never been any worship between the young man and his father.

Groaning, Jared stood up and continued to watch as the waves crashed against the ocean liner. Someone knocked on the cabin door, and Jared jumped, startled. "Just a minute," he called out and went to the door. He withdrew a small pistol from under his jacket and swung the door open in less than a second. Seconds later, he pulled the intruder inside and slammed the door behind them, locking it without hesitation.

Jared kept the gun squared at the person's chest, patting him down, searching for any weapons. The new arrival raised their hands in surprise and surrender. An amused grin etched across the person's face, and they laughed. It was a low, guttural, and mirthless sound. "Is that any way to greet a ship's captain, Mr. Saviano?"

Jared scowled and holstered the gun. "Don't talk down to me, Alex," he replied, shaking his head. "I am in no mood for your sardonic wit. I assume you know why I am here?" he asked. Turning to the minibar, he retrieved two glasses, filling each with ice and liquor. He handed one to the man before him and sat on the edge of the bed behind them with a soft thump.

"Yes, I know why you are here. I'm not stupid," Alex replied. His eyes flashed with slight disdain, but his voice stayed neutral. "You came on board with the pretense of a vacation. But somebody sent you. Your orders were explicit. Come, do the job and get out before they discover you." Alex Mackenzie's words were mechanical, as though he were reading from a script. He took a sip of liquor, watching the other man over the brim of the glass through half-closed eyes. "Is that correct?"

Jared grunted. "That is an excellent description of why I am here, yes. Do you know where he is right now?" He got right to the point. There was not much time for idle chitchat; too many lives were at stake.

Alex's eyes opened. He smiled. "Yes, he's doing what he does every time he comes on board, Jared. Your father is in the casino. He is squandering away his fortune on the slot machines. He plans to go to the blackjack room next." Bitterness dripped from his words as he spoke. He hated the man, but he was powerless to do anything to stop Jack.

Jared chuckled. The laughter did not reach his eyes, though. "Blackjack for Jack, huh?" He smiled and fingered the pistol. "Well, then why don't we go see how much my father has stolen from this beautiful ship?" He downed his drink in one gulp. The pair slipped into the ship's corridor without another word.

Jared had followed his father's moves from afar for several months. He was part of a group of people who worked behind the scenes, maneuvering events to what they believed to be the best outcomes for all involved. There was no "official" name for this group of people. But they called themselves the "Cleanup Crew." While they included many occupations in the community, the group of men and women stayed anonymous. They worked for no one, and yet they did for everyone. There were members of the "Cleanup Crew" in all walks and professions of society, from top government officials to the local grocery stores. They recruited Jared as a member when he was eighteen.

When Jack found out Jared wanted to join The Crew, he was furious. In his eyes, they worked to achieve everything Jack abhorred. The Crew was notorious for following the laws of justice. The police were their primary source of support. Jack was not completely against law and order; in fact, several prominent police officers were in his pocket. But because he worked above the law, he could not trust the police or Jared.

Jack's final straw with Jared was when he refused to stay home and take care of his sister. He was the oldest of the Saviano children, the result of a short-term fling between Jack and a woman he'd met not long after marrying Patricia. The woman became pregnant. Patricia found out and gave Jack an ultimatum. Although he promised to sever all ties with the woman, he still funneled whatever extra money he made into her bank account. Patricia agreed to raise Jared as hers, but on the stipulation that Jack was not to tell Jared who his birth mother was. But when Jared turned twenty-one, he mysteriously discovered the truth anyway. After confronting his father, the two argued and agreed to never speak to each other again. Jared left for good.

Daniel encountered his half-brother once as a young man, but he doubted Jared remembered the meeting. Later, he found Patricia's locket, with Jared's photograph, in a drawer by accident and asked her about it. Patricia denied everything at first but then told the whole story. She made Daniel promise not to tell Jack he knew about his half-brother.

Chapter 32

The Past

Jack was tired of running. He had all but given up on the destiny he believed fate had deemed for him. His son Daniel was, in his eyes, the epitome of all Jack detested. "Where did I go wrong with you, Daniel?" Jack asked himself in a whisper full of heartbreaking regret. Jack was a murderer and adulterer many times over, who had vowed long ago that he would control people. Daniel's decision to become a lawman had estranged father and son.

Jack recalled with a half-smile the first time he encountered the infamous *La Cosa Nostra*—the mafia. Its head's name was Anton Savantini. Anton had recently divorced when he encountered the then twelve-year-old Jack, who would idolize him and his way of life. The divorce was amicable, except that Anton later set in motion a plan to kill his ex-wife and take total control of all assets the couple had accumulated. To him, meeting the boy was a blessing in disguise. Anton planned to use Jack as a patsy in the plot.

Anton was dying. He knew it, and his friends and family knew it. Soon, his multimillion-dollar empire would crumble and fall. It was just a matter of time. Time was a luxury the man did not have. When Anton's wife discovered the truth about her "perfect" husband, she threatened to leave him and promised to take his son away from him. Anton swore on a stack of Bibles that he would make his wife pay for what she did.

When Anton met Jack, he knew he found who he needed to help him carry out his revenge. Jack was no fool—Anton realized it from studying the young boy for a month. He knew Jack hated his parents for being interracial. He saw that the teenager seethed with hatred for them. He wanted to bring Jack into the fold, and he vowed the teenager would be his.

Jack felt the eyes of the older man on him for weeks. At first, he assumed Anton was a dirty man lusting after him. Then, one day after church, the man followed Jack and his parents and approached them. As they were getting in their car, Jack realized Anton wanted something from him. It made the young boy uncomfortable.

Anton had explained to Jack's parents that he was a retired teacher of philosophy and had gone through a messy and long separation. Because of the divorce, he lost contact with his own child, who he had been teaching philosophy, and he hoped he could pass his knowledge on to another young man instead. Charles, a man of science with a strict religious upbringing, was ecstatic at the opportunity his son would have.

The following week, Jack went to Anton's house. For the next two years, Anton taught him all he would need to

163

know about "modern philosophy." Anton died three months before Jack's more formal induction into *La Cosa Nostra*.

Chapter 33

The Present

Jack looked down at a photograph on the table. He had come back to his cabin, removed his clothes, showered, and then slipped into his favorite pair of flannel pajamas. When he was younger, he slept in nothing more than the bedsheets. As he grew older, he yielded to a sense of modesty.

Taking a calculated breath, Jack grabbed the photograph and studied it. It was taken at a banquet about forty years earlier. He didn't know then, nor did he know now, why they chose him for the award. Yet, he felt this picture was a testimony to his undeniable greatness. The men flanking him were smiling; their arms were around him as if they were protecting him. Jack had felt uncomfortable in his tuxedo, but he remembered Patricia insisted he look his best. The award he clutched in his white-knuckled grasp was as inconsequential to him as the banquet.

The most significant part of the photograph to Jack was the person seated at the far end of the table, out of view. He knew the person was there at the time, attempting to blend in with the crowd. Jack laughed at her almost standoffish appearance. How his mother had gotten there, not even he knew, but he found her presence a comfort. Now that Leah had spared his life in the alleyway, Jack realized that his mother had been his sole supporter through the years. He had long ago realized that Charles was his betrayer.

Charles had originally tried to forbid his son from attending that the banquet, realizing that Jack was entwined with the mafia. But Jack went anyway, and he threatened to shoot Charles on sight if he dared show his face there. That was why Jack had ordered his father's murder. It was not because Charles revealed Leah was an undercover agent, although that piece of information was valuable. No, it was because Charles had betrayed Jack by not supporting him. He had to learn that the punishment was death.

"Are you certain you don't regret killing your father?" a voice said, cutting through the quiet of the empty room. "You can try to convince almost anyone you enjoyed killing him, but I know better."

Jack realized he had been speaking aloud while looking at the photograph. A small chuckle erupted from somewhere in the shadows, and Jack sucked in a breath, startled. "Why are *you* here?" Jack demanded once he could find his voice. He studied the new arrival for a moment while tossing the photograph back onto the table.

Standing, Jack leaned back against the wall. He noticed the gun concealed under the man's jacket and chuckled dryly. "Ah," he grinned, "I see. You have come to finish your brother Daniel's botched-up job." Spreading his hands outward, Jack leveled his gaze at his oldest son. "So, tell me what's stopping you, Jared."

"I wouldn't risk killing you here." Jared shook his head firmly. "My boss would not want your vile blood all over this fine establishment." Looking out the small porthole, the younger Saviano noticed that the afternoon sky was clear; any sign of inclement weather had all but disappeared out into the middle of the sea. "No, I am here to *warn* you." Jared lowered his hand toward his hidden weapon and sighed. "It's not safe for you, Dad." Jared hoped his father would understand the full implication of his words. "The Crew sent me to warn you. They have been watching everything and told me to get you somewhere safe. It's too dangerous for you right now. They consider you a great asset to their cause since you dispose of other criminals."

The senior Saviano laughed. His mustache twitched as he answered: "Not safe, boy?" Raising his eyes to the ceiling, Jack nodded to a black globe above them and shrugged. "What the hell do you suppose that is? There are surveillance cameras all over the place. No one would dare do anything—they would get their ass handed to them. That's why I boarded the ship." He clapped his son's shoulder with a hand. "You worry too much!" Jack added.

"Fine," Jared hissed under his breath, letting his hand drop from his weapon. "Have it your way, you bastard! Remember: I tried to warn you! Someone else is following and watching you, not just The Crew. Someone knows your secrets, old man, and intends them to remain secret. They already killed mom, and don't say you did it either. The Crew saw everything."

Jack blinked in surprise. "I don't think we should talk here anymore. I'll meet you in your cabin in ten minutes, and we will discuss what to do." Jack then acknowledged the captain, who had stayed quiet since the start of the conversation. "Alex? You know what to do, I am sure, so go. You have a ship to run, or have you forgotten your duty?"

At Jack's words, Alex shifted from one foot to the other, his gaze dropping to the floor. "I've not forgotten," he mumbled, embarrassed. Jack had long had him in his pocket. "You need anything before I go, sir?" He kept his voice neutral, like he and Jack Saviano were strangers when, in reality, they had known each other for years. Still, Alex always felt Jack would sooner end the association with a bullet to the back of his head than continue with their "friendship." *If you were not my boss, Jack, I would kill you*, he thought, turning to leave.

Jack shrugged, and then he shook his head. "No, Captain, I am set. Have a pleasant evening!" The expression on the mobster's face betrayed the joy in his voice. He added, "Cross me, and you won't live to see the sun rise."

Jack allowed a tiny smile to touch his lips and then clapped his oldest son on the shoulder. "Shall we go?" Unmitigated terror crept through the younger man's entire body. Jared had the distinct impression he would be the one to die in the next few hours rather than Jack, but he didn't know why he felt that way. All he knew for sure was that he needed to get in touch with Daniel to warn him, too.

* * *

Dan's apartment phone was ringing, but he let the machine catch it. He was exhausted, having had only four hours of sleep. His mother was dead, and his father's body had disappeared. But it was something else that still troubled him.

Dan lay on the bed, his hands folded over his chest. With his eyes closed, he replayed his father's last moments until it seemed like a video had recorded the horrific event. He saw the look of disgust in the older man's eyes seconds after the bullet struck his chest. He imagined Jack clutching at the spot to stop the blood from escaping.

Then, in his mind's eye, from the far corner of the alley, Daniel saw something he hadn't noticed. A figure stood behind the lamppost in the shadows. Beyond that, there was utter blackness at the far end of the alley. This person leaned against the wall, arms across their chest. Why Dan hadn't noticed they weren't alone before, he wasn't sure. His memory had betrayed him again.

Until then, Dan's knowledge of the incident was that no one else except his father and Leah had been there. So, who was the solitary figure hiding there, watching the events as they happened? Why hadn't whoever it was come to their aid? These and a million more unanswered questions echoed in Daniel's mind as he fell into a profound, nightmare-filled sleep.

Later, Dan awoke with a start, his forehead and face covered with beads of sweat. The remnants of the last nightmare left his memory as he struggled to sit. Visions of his father dressed as the Grim Reaper and, to a lesser extent, Jack the Ripper lingered in his brain. The last image was no surprise to Dan because Jack shared his name with the infamous murderer of the last part of the nineteenth century.

Dan heard the familiar sound of his answering machine beeping. The noise floated up the stairway into his bedroom, and he frowned as it registered in his mind. Daniel remembered someone had called him before he fell asleep, but now it seemed surreal to him as he went downstairs. Glancing down, it chagrined Dan to notice he had not removed his clothes.

Finding out the truth about his family had taken its toll. On cue, Dan's stomach rumbled, and he chuckled, remembering he had not eaten since early yesterday afternoon. Dan crossed the living room, grabbed the leftover takeout from the refrigerator, and sat on the couch. The food was still in the container he had brought home and, not bothering to heat it, he ate straight from the carton. He found yesterday's newspaper on the table to his right and wondered who put it there. Daniel had not remembered bringing it into the apartment, nor did he recall having read it. Eating, he thumbed through the paper, chuckling at the comics. He grimaced as he learned about the latest fiasco the President was facing.

Daniel was not one for political affairs; his father discouraged the family from indulging in such ridiculous associations. As a young man, Dan had asked his father if he could register to vote. Jack's response of "no, politics is a game best played by fools and the weak-minded" surprised Dan. How could someone who grew up in Arizona's suburbs and, to a lesser extent, Illinois not be interested in state affairs? There were, of course, rumors that the elder Saviano had been active in most government elections, supporting some less prominent candidates to get them in his pocket. But Dan had never seen his father in photographs with any politicians or celebrities. All he recalled was a picture taken at a banquet about forty years earlier.

Daniel had been a young boy at the time, so he couldn't join his family at the awards banquet. But years later, someone confessed the banquet was in his father's honor. No one told Daniel why his father had been the chosen recipient of the prestigious award. Dan only saw the photograph once, but recognizing his father as one of the people in the picture, Dan had asked Leah about the photograph's origins. She simply shrugged and changed the topic. Jack had been holding a plaque, but in the photograph, the words on the plaque had faded and blurred, Dan assumed from the passage of time. Hindsight suggested a different tale.

Dan now realized that Leah must have altered the photograph to hide the truth from her grandson. Jack had likely ordered her to do so, to save his son from discovering the truth behind his family roots with the mafia. Many times, Leah had begged him to tell Daniel the truth, but he refused to do so. When Leah later approached Daniel about the family secret herself, she felt a big weight lift from her shoulders.

Dan was growing anxious as the day wore on. Since their trip to the warehouse the previous night, his grandmother hadn't talked to him, and Dan began to worry. It was true that he had not heard from her for many years before that without worry. But that had never concerned him since he thought she had died of a heart attack. Now that he knew his grandmother was alive and well, Dan felt nervous about having not heard from her.

Tossing the newspaper aside, Dan rubbed the bridge of his nose. Drawing in a deep breath, he reached for his cell phone on the side table, where he had plugged it in to charge when he had returned home. With trembling hands, he dialed the number Leah had given him. After several rings and voicemail picking up, Dan left a message telling Leah to call him back. All he could do now was wait for her to contact him.

As Dan stood to toss his plate in the trash, he remembered the beep from the answering machine, and he noticed the light on the machine was blinking. Taking a breath, he pressed the button that would play the unheard message. As he heard the robotic voice on the machine, he trembled. "I thought I told you to leave the past alone, Danny. It's time to pay the fiddler! Your mother was the first example. If you don't want someone else to be your next lesson, I suggest you back off from the past and let sleeping dogs lie!"

Chapter 34

The Past

They murdered this victim like the others. The difference this time was that the killer felt *extreme* remorse. The killing was no longer thrilling. Watching the dying victims now gave the killer a sense of sorrow. The victim was naked like the rest, her once ample bosom now splayed open, internal organs tossed about inside her.

Lauren was bloody and wounded from the torture she had withstood over the previous two hours. She was still alive for the final twenty minutes but could not move or scream. She knew what was happening to her. This was the crucial difference between her and the earlier victims. Why the killer used Rohypnol on her, no one would ever know. Her once happy, shiny brown eyes were now lifeless. The murderer wanted her. They *needed* her, to try to revive their need for arousal.

The killer stared down into the still-open eyes, which were nothing more than an empty abyss of darkness. "My poor Lauren." The killer ran their finger across the blood-soaked blade and shook their head. "You could have lived a long, beautiful, and happy life. If you listened to your conscience and stayed the hell away from me, I wouldn't have been able to seduce and kill you."

Rocking back and forth on their heels, the killer let the knife slip free and clatter against the linoleum floor. Grief overcame them, and a tear slid from their eye. They wrapped their arms tighter around their body as they shuddered from more unshed tears. There was no choice now, they knew. Nobody could bring Lauren McKay back to life. And no one could wash away the memories, pains, and desires of the killer. It was Jack's fault the murderer was this way.

Chapter 35

The Present

Sara Saviano leaned back against the leather couch and kicked off her shoes. She had come back to the hotel room after her mother's funeral, hoping nobody had seen her there. She had kept her composure throughout the ordeal, shedding only the tears she felt necessary. Sara despised her mother; she hated the fact that the woman had been so nonchalant about her being the product of an affair. Sara knew Jack was not her father. Since the discovery, she made plans to ruin the many people behind the lies in their family.

It had taken years of planning, but Sara knew it was now time. Nothing else mattered to her. She would rather die than let the duplicity continue. The woman she and her foolish brother had called their mother was dead. Sara thanked God himself for that, though she had long ago abandoned any true religious beliefs. Having no religious beliefs helped her feel she could better understand and admit she was gay.

Sara straightened upward, allowing her feet to touch the floor. The all-too-familiar tingle crept down her legs, and she knew her feet had fallen asleep. Flinching, she bit back a sob as she struggled to endure the pins and needles feeling in her feet. Reaching into her pocket, Sara pulled out her wallet and opened it. The picture was still where she had placed it several months ago. It was taken over the summer, during a journey to Mexico.

Chapter 36

The Past

Miriam and Sara had returned from a horseback riding excursion. They were about to board their ship when a tour guide stopped them and offered to take their picture. In the photograph, the couple was obviously smitten with each other. A week later, Miriam had approached Sara, who was fixing dinner, with a feeble excuse to end their liaison. "I can't continue this way. You know I love you, though, and I always will." She sighed, looked Sara in the eyes, and continued, "Circumstances change, as you well know. I think it's time for us. I don't get to see you anymore, even at work. And speaking of work . . ." Miriam hesitated, trying to find the right words to explain. She finished with, "Esther Martinelli called me yesterday while you were on your lunch break. She wants me to join her firm as a partner."

The words came out in a hurried jumble, which almost convinced Sara that she heard them wrong. "What?! You cannot be serious! We have been partners for years! You want to . . . You want to leave the firm and me because of some female who wears flashy clothes and drives a sixty-thousand-dollar car?" Sara's eyes widened with anger at each word. Her breath came out in heaves. She was hyperventilating, and the kitchen spun.

Sara felt she would faint. But an instant later, she experienced a clarity she had never before felt. Her movements were precise as she pressed against the drawer behind her. As if in a trance, she pulled her arm forward, sliding the drawer open. A steak knife was in her hand an instant later. The cold metal turned from ice to heat in seconds as it came toward the woman standing near Sara. "No," Sara whispered, "you will not leave me. No one *ever* leaves me."

The serrated blade hit its precise target in the center of Miriam's chest as she instinctively raised her arms to try to fend off the unexpected attack. Trying to stop Sara was futile, though. Miriam was on the kitchen floor a moment later. Sara's free hand slid around Miriam's neck, cutting off her air, causing her to suffocate. As the knife pierced her flesh, Miriam tried to cry out. The pressure on her throat was unbearable. *Oh God, somebody help me!* she prayed. But Miriam realized nobody was coming to help. As the knife blade slid free of her twisted flesh, she took her last breath.

Sara, filled with bloodlust from the kill, felt sated. There was one last step, though. The ones responsible for Sara's actions had to die, she resolved. Rising to her feet, she set the knife on the kitchen counter without washing it off. She made herself a sandwich, ate, and went to take a shower. After washing the blood and gore from her body,

179

Sara stood over Miriam's body, shaking her head. "I told you," she whispered to the corpse that was once her lover and best friend, "you would not leave me."

* * *

Two weeks later, Sara opened her eyes and blinked several times, rubbing at the bridge of her nose. When she wrenched her hand away, she felt her cheeks soaked with tears. She was sobbing, she realized with a whimper. She had been doing that a lot the past several months as the memories returned. Sara despised what she had become; she hated the emotions she was feeling. Sara was becoming a feeble and sniveling woman.

Glancing over at the kitchen floor, it pleased Sara to notice the bloodstains where Miriam's body had fallen weeks before were gone. *It was a stupid accident*, she repeated in her brain until it became a mantra. She almost believed it to be true, too. The technical term was plausible deniability, she recalled, laughing at herself.

Sara had suffered so much mental and physical anguish throughout her life. She longed to be healthy, to walk carefree among her friends and peers, and to not have them stare at her because she used a cane to help her walk. Yet, she knew this could never be, and it made her bitter beyond human understanding. Sara wanted to destroy the impure thoughts racing through her head like demons from the bowels of Hell. When she considered all she had experienced during her existence, she swore she was already in Hell.

To say Sara despised her parents was not an over-statement. She wished them dead for the physical and mental torture they inflicted on her. She felt she had no real identity except her name. She had no sense of belonging, no knowledge of who she was as a person. She longed for the touch of someone willing to give her not only a sexual identity but the release of her emotional captivity.

Even at an early age, Sara sensed she preferred the embrace of a female against her body. But Jack and Patricia had discouraged sexual desires for anyone except for men. Jack insisted Sara stay at home during her teenage years. Patricia had little choice but to consent to the arrangement. If she tried to disagree, he flew into a fury that terrified her and the children.

Too often, Sara recalled, she and Daniel would escape to their rooms, slamming and locking their doors behind them in terror. Both would fall into a nightmare-filled slumber and wake up the next morning drained and exhausted. Sara didn't realize Daniel would not suffer the same mental state she did—Daniel wouldn't vow vengeance against Jack, Patricia, and anyone else who had hurt him. Nor did Sara fully comprehend her own raw emotions, her soul yearning to be set free from the emotional agony she suffered as her sanity waned. Sara did not recall her first victim's name, only that she felt alive when cutting her throat.

Sara learned early in her life that the only one she could depend on was herself. She knew it was impossible to trust anyone else. *It was trusting people which led to lies, betrayal, and . . . rage*, she convinced herself. Before her first kill, Sara kept her emotions in check, refusing to allow anyone to get close to her, and she hated it when she lost control. But after the second murder, bloodlust took over, which was then replaced by adrenaline, and then a restless yearning to kill again. This cycle went on for years; the death toll seemed incalculable, at least to authorities. But Sara herself kept meticulous records on her crimes. She had murdered thirty-four women in her teenage years alone.

Sara rose to her feet, walked over to the spot where her lover had fallen, and squatted. She took a deep breath. She could still smell the stench of bleach and dried blood. Sara cleaned the spot as best as she could. Yet, no matter how hard she tried, she could not wash the stain away. The scent was both intoxicating and disgusting to her, yet Sara regretted nothing. Given the opportunity, she would do it again. *No one left her—ever. If they tried, they would pay.*

Sara smiled as she remembered what she had done with the corpse. Using the high-powered blender Miriam gave her as a gift, she pulverized the body into liquid form and used it to make a protein shake. After a moment, she turned and opened the refrigerator. She needed a drink.

Chapter 37

The Past

Sara fought to sit up in her bed. With some effort, she swung her feet to the floor and pushed herself to a sitting position. To her chagrin, she noticed her curtains were open. She grunted under her breath, shaking her head in annoyance at the sight. A fresh blanket of snow lay on the ground. With another grunt, she grabbed her cane that was on the floor. She hated what she was, even at thirteen. She had grown weaker in the past several months. But she knew she had to put up a decent facade for her parents, to prove she would mature.

Smiling, Sara glimpsed at the picture on the nightstand beside her bed. Someone took the photograph at the local mall two weeks earlier. In the photo, Sara sat in her wheelchair wearing a dark purple pantsuit. Standing behind her were her best friends, Candace Winters and Miriam. The latter rested her hand on Sara's shoulder, squeezing it seconds before the photographer snapped the photo. Sara had felt a shiver of excitement at the touch. She had never felt that way about anyone, and she gasped. Miriam said nothing about it to Sara, so Sara wondered if her friend felt the same reaction she had. She dared not say anything, though, for fear she was incorrect.

Later that day, Sara and Miriam went into the bathroom together. After they were inside, Miriam turned toward Sara, put her hand on Sara's shoulder, and then lay her other hand under Sara's legs, preparing to raise her from the transport chair. Once more, Sara felt a spark of electricity, and she blushed. It was not from embarrassment but from excitement at the contact.

The two young women gazed into each other's eyes for a long, silent moment, surprise registering first on Miriam's face and then Sara's. Miriam grinned. Then, by pure impulse, she pulled Sara closer, sweeping her hand against Sara's back and down. Moments afterward, their lips met, and Sara gave in to the need she had denied for several years.

After what seemed like an eternity of passion, both teenagers came back to themselves, remembering where they were. "No regrets?" Miriam whispered into Sara's ear as she pulled back. Sara smiled and allowed Miriam to help her back into the chair. The bond between the two young women had started as quickly as it later ended.

Chapter 38

The Present

The ship had returned to the dock and had been there for less than an hour. Jack stayed on board in his cabin, thankful no one had disturbed him. The ship was from his private fleet. That was one of the many benefits of being a man with some authority. Jared left the ship hours earlier and returned to wherever it was he had come from. Jack was thankful that his oldest son was nowhere near since he had enough to deal with already.

The thought of Jared tracking him down to warn him of his impending death was amusing to Jack. He had taken care of himself for the better part of his sixty-plus years. Jack had lived through countless death threats and assassination attempts and even a severe heart attack. The latest effort was no different. He thought about the people who betrayed him over the years and admitted he missed a few of the ones he had disposed of. With a groan, he ran a hand across his face, annoyed to feel his fingertips were wet when he drew back.

Patricia—God, what have I done? What kind of monster did I turn our daughter into? Questions played over in Jack's mind until a moan bubbled up from his chest, and he could no longer hold back the tears. He loved Patricia. Her betrayal wounded him to the point he had gone in search of other women to give him back what she had taken from him, but they meant nothing to him. He had realized Patricia was cheating when he discovered that Sara was not his daughter. It paid to have spies and contacts keeping him in the loop.

At first, Jack considered confronting his wife about her affairs, but then he realized he was no better than Patricia at keeping vows of faithfulness. He had to accept the truth. He loved Sara as his own. He kept a close eye on her over the years once he realized she was possessive and physically aggressive as far as what she had and with whom she had it. The former possessiveness was not as dangerous, he felt, as the latter physical aggressiveness. He tried to cloister her as much as he could when she hit puberty, but the girl was as hotheaded as he was.

When the homicides began, Jack realized too late what he had done in trying to shelter Sara from the outside world because of her condition. It had caused the young woman to become even more aggressive, possessive, and obsessive. She started slipping out at night and returning before dawn the next morning, before her parents would wake. She had learned to trick her friends into taking her to various nightclubs and parties. Jack suspected as much. Yet, he had no evidence. He did, however, come into her bedroom and discover bloodied sheets.

From then on, Jack recorded everything Sara did. At

first, he assumed Sara had been slipping out to meet a boy. He ordered one of his team members to follow her to and from school and wherever else she asked to go. Around that time, Jack commissioned a group of architects to build a hidden passageway between his children's rooms. He hoped it would not come to having to seal Sara's room completely—which it never did.

Jack left his cabin and passed through the ocean liner's now empty hallways with a weary groan. The silence surrounding him was almost overpowering, yet he had to concentrate on planning his next move. Events from the past several days flooded his memory, and he closed his eyes, praying for a little solace. His wife was dead, the victim of a monster far more cunning than he was.

Jack turned down the adjoining hallway, ending in the deck's central area. The elevators were ahead of him. Jack considered his next move, glancing up at the plaque on the wall that displayed the ship's layout. He realized this was an intricate chess game as he studied the map.

Rubbing the flesh where the bullet penetrated his chest days before, Jack squinted his eyes, focusing. He pictured his daughter as a child, a rebellious teenager, and a woman hell-bent on killing him. *What are you planning now, you little devil?* he wondered. Jack suddenly realized exactly what Sara planned to do. *Dammit! She wants to kill Daniel! I must warn him somehow. I can't keep hiding any longer. We may be on opposite sides of the law, but what could happen to me is nothing compared to what she will do if she finds him!*

Jack was already sprinting toward the walkway of the ship when his cell phone rang. He reached into his pants pocket and flipped the phone open as he ran. Not bothering with formality, he barked, "What are you doing, you little asshole?" He bit his lip as he almost flew off the gangplank onto the street level below him. Sweat poured from his face and forehead, but he didn't bother to wipe it away.

Sara chuckled. "I am carrying out my revenge, Father. You took all I loved in the world. Now you and your bastard son will pay!" Sara hung up the phone after muttering a phrase that told Jack what he could do to himself.

Jack was on an airplane to Arizona within the hour. He realized Sara had called his cell phone. His jaw dropped in confusion. *How did she know he was still alive?*

Chapter 39

The Near Present

It stopped snowing twenty minutes earlier. The snow was a bizarre sight for Arizona at the start of November. Jack never liked the snow as a boy. His opinion still hadn't changed. Why he came back here, not even he knew. His mother, of all people, called him a week before and said they needed to talk. Leah was weary of their estrangement and wanted to make amends.

Jack hadn't suspected the sudden change of heart in the woman. He recalled the last time they had seen each other: the night the FBI had taken his children from him. Jack vowed vengeance, swearing if he ever saw her again, he would kill her. Even today, after so many years, the rage and bitterness still consumed him.

Jack was sitting in the corner booth at Denny's. A half-full glass of root beer and a plate of bacon, eggs, and toast were on the table when Leah stepped into the restaurant. Their eyes met, and for a moment, Jack panicked. The realization he was afraid of his mother was a jolt to him; nothing ever scared him.

It took a minute for Leah to follow the host to the table. Jack seemed to have aged a hundred years. Leah studied her son as she sat across from him. He looked pale and skinny to her, and his bright eyes had dulled. She thought she was staring at a different person than her son. Leah took a deep breath and exhaled before speaking. "Hello, Jack," she whispered. Her voice was calm, although she was more than a little nervous about seeing him. "It's been a long time," she continued.

Jack set his fork down and glanced at her. "Leah," he said, "please relax." He turned his attention back to his food as she ordered an Oreo milkshake and bacon cheeseburger.

They sat in silence for a while until Leah spoke. "You know why I'm here, Jack," she said. Reaching under her jacket, she produced a sealed Manila envelope. She slid it across the table. His mother sucked in a breath, waiting for him to move.

When Jack did move, his movements were measured and methodical. He opened the metal clasp with a soft snap. His eyes met Leah's intense gaze as he took out several documents and pictures. "Where did you find these?" Several of the papers were documents he had written decades ago, but there was another document that caught his eye. It was addressed to Patricia from the doctor who had delivered Sara. Jack's eyes widened as he scanned the letter. "What the hell?" he muttered to himself. His jaw relaxed, and he stared at Leah, waiting for her to speak. He tossed the paper at her, and she jumped. "So, you know about this?" he asked. His tone was accusatory.

Leah's mouth worked for several seconds as she read

the words. She remembered the doctor who wrote the letter to Patricia committed suicide shortly after writing it. Patricia had tried to dispose of the letter, but Leah retrieved it for her files on the Saviano family. Leah sighed and nodded. "Dennis knew you weren't Sara's birth father. The knowledge weighed on his shoulders and on Patricia's. He wanted to tell you, but Patricia begged him not to. I convinced her it would hurt you more."

Leah shook her head. She was about to continue when the server brought her food. He put it down in front of her and then left them alone. Leah reached for the ketchup bottle, pouring ketchup on the side of the plate. When she finished, she took a large bite and chewed. She said nothing more for a few minutes, letting Jack absorb her words.

The revelation stunned Jack. *He was really not Sara's father.* Jack had long suspected as much, but there was no conclusive evidence until now, and he was embarrassed that it seemed everyone else had already known. His mouth and throat had gone dry as he read the words on the paper in front of him. He gulped his drink.

Jack frowned, reached for the other documents, and rifled through them as he waited for his mother to say something. His eyes skimmed over the pages. It astonished him to learn that Leah had somehow also found and copied his notes about Sara that he kept hidden in his private office. A sad smile touched Leah's lips. "I know everything," she said, reading Jack's thoughts. "You were right about Sara all along."

A figure loomed to Jack's right. He turned and looked

to see who it was. His "dead" wife, Patricia, stood in front of him. Her eyes flashed in the light. "Hello, Jack," she said with mock cheerfulness as she dropped into the booth next to Leah. "Isn't this a lovely family reunion?"

Chapter 40

The Present

Sara was tired of running away, but she knew if she stopped, it would end for her. Long ago, she learned to manage her epilepsy (caused by hydrocephalus), yet her body would still succumb to occasional seizures. It wore her out. But she remained overwhelmed with the intense desire to kill.

When Sara first recognized she couldn't resist committing murder, she assumed it was necessary to help her achieve a sexual release. Back then, it was all about survival. She killed to survive, to keep her secrets buried. But soon enough, it was no longer about self-preservation. It was about the *joy* it brought her. To put it bluntly, it turned her on watching people die, looking at them begging *in vain* for their lives.

Sara fingered the knife, still crusted with Miriam's blood months after the murder. She had enjoyed killing her lover, but now wished she hadn't done it. Now, she longed for the delicate, comforting feel of her lover's body against hers. But that could never be, thanks to Sara's impetuous nature. *You foolish and wretched excuse of a woman! You couldn't let it go, could you?* she thought to herself. For a moment, Sara wondered if she was scolding herself or Miriam for interfering and causing the predicament. Neither one mattered now. The deed was done, and her lover was gone. For the first time in Sara's life, she was completely alone, and it frightened her.

Vengeance is mine, Sara thought, smiling as she dropped the knife to the glass coffee table in front of her. She climbed to her feet. She wanted a drink. Using her cane for support, Sara made her way toward the kitchenette of the hotel room. She seized a small bottle of Pepsi from the cabinet and drained it into a glass.

Sara did not bother putting ice in the glass as she hated cold soda. Instead, she took two or three long gulps of the cola and then grabbed the bottle. Carrying the cup and bottle to the coffee table, she placed both on the tabletop. It would be a long day, and when it was over, she would make sure all the loose ends were tied up. Jack would have to die first, to lure Dan in. Then she would take care of the brother who abandoned her all those years ago.

* * *

Jack struggled to open his eyes. Wiping at them with his hand, he realized he did not recognize where he was. He couldn't remember where he'd been for the last several hours.

A few minutes went by, and Jack's vision came into focus. The last thing he remembered was leaving Sky Harbor Airport and starting the hour and a half long journey back to Prescott by shuttle. Jack had fallen asleep. When he woke up on the shuttle, he recognized Sara sitting in the aisle seat across from him. She was grinning at him. Winking at him, she lowered her gaze to her lap. A small pistol rested there, just out of sight of the other passengers.

So much had happened in the previous days and weeks—from Leah contacting him to the revelation that his wife was still alive to her unexpected murder at their former home and more. So, it wasn't too strange to hear an all-too-familiar voice on his cell phone when Sara called and said she was coming after him. She had been the shadowy figure watching the scene unfold in the alleyway—the figure Dan later recalled seeing—so, she saw Leah help Jack and figured he was still alive. Now, she had followed him from the airport and slipped onto the shuttle without him noticing. When the shuttle stopped to drop Jack off, Sara followed him and cold-cocked the aging man before he could drive away.

Sara brought Jack to the same warehouse where he murdered his own father—at least, thought he did. Jack now knew for certain that Sara was not his child. She was the offspring of the treacherous liar he married. Yet, he had still claimed Sara as his own. And he was grateful Patricia let it happen. Had he known, however, that Sara would turn into an abomination, Jack would have made sure someone dealt with her long ago.

Jack focused once more on his surroundings, wincing as he examined the room. A brilliant yellow light shone above him. Off to his right, he heard a small scuffling sound, and he sucked in a breath. A rat scurried across the linoleum floor. Jack grunted as he tried to move his hands upward to shield his eyes from the light. He realized he was tied to a wooden chair, his feet fastened to the legs. "What the hell is going on here?!" he cried out, thankful he was not gagged.

When no one responded, Jack fought against his bindings. After several attempts at freeing himself, he realized his captor made the restraints so tight, any effort to free himself would hurt him more. Jack cursed. His eyes were growing heavy again. He tried to call out, and once more, no reply came. He was in a warehouse, he realized, to his dismay. Another rat scurried across the floor, and he heard a soft creak. A door was opening. "Someone help me!" Jack called out, hoping whoever had come in was there to save him.

Jack's hopes died a second later when he heard a reply. "Shut up, old man! No one is here, and your son won't know to come here until I call him. For now, we are alone." Jack heard a soft chuckle, and then the voice continued in a menacing whisper: "I'd say it is rather appropriate for you to die here, in the same place you murdered your father." Sara laughed.

Jack tried to scream but was met with a hard slap to his face. A second later, darkness overtook him once more.

* * *

Still at his apartment after having listened to the menacing voicemail message he received, Daniel gulped the ice water he was drinking. Though he had been with Leah the night before—when she showed him the locket—it seemed like ages had passed since he'd seen her. Dan reflected on the events leading to this moment. He had lost both his parents in less than forty-eight hours—or so he thought. And the long-lost sister he located had vanished again. She had not contacted anyone at her office in days.

When Dan had received the caller's voicemail message, things came into focus for him. He reread the meticulous files Leah kept about Sara. They left an unpleasant taste in his mouth. The papers seemed to describe Sara as a lesbian and a psychopath. And their father had apparently insisted she stay under close observation throughout her teenage years so that she could not escape his watchful eye.

Daniel finished the rest of his water with a weary and troubled sigh. He did not know where his sister was and had no further contact with Leah. Jack was dead; he killed him. So, it appeared no one could stop his sister from making her next move: coming after him. With a grunt of pain, he dropped his glass in the kitchen sink. Daniel did not understand what to do next or where to go.

As if someone had been reading his thoughts, Dan's cell phone rang. Startled, he cursed as he stubbed his toe against the cabinet door under the sink. "Shit!" he yelled and yanked open his phone. "Yeah? What do you want?"

he hissed.

"It's time, Dan. It's time for you to *die*!" the caller said in a bitter reply. "Our family reunion, brother, dear, is imminent. Come back to the warehouse. I assume you know the one? . . . Good. You have fifteen minutes left to live."

* * *

Daniel Saviano climbed out of the driver's seat of his unmarked patrol car. He slammed the door, locking it with a resigned expression. He felt he could not stop the lunatic inside the building, but he knew he had to try. Slipping his car keys into his pants pocket, Daniel looked up into the night sky. At least a foot and a half of snow still covered the ground outside the warehouse. He knew the abandoned warehouse must be freezing.

Daniel said nothing to anyone on the police force about knowing his sister's location. He told no one at the department where he was going or what he'd been doing. For that, he felt guilty. But Daniel's superiors would accuse him of obstruction of justice if he alerted anyone. Daniel knew in his heart he should put duty before honor. But he couldn't care less about department policy at that moment. He knew what his sister was doing, and he knew she wouldn't go down without a fight, taking everyone with her.

Because of that, Daniel had left a voicemail message for Leah, telling her about the call he received from his sister less than half an hour before. He promised her he would be on alert, but he insisted on going alone. Daniel wasn't stupid, though. Tucked inside its holster was his police-issued pistol. He also carried several more hidden guns and various other items intended to shield him from the inevitable attack that awaited him. Shivering—he was not sure whether from the chill in the air or fear—Daniel opened the door to the warehouse and went inside.

The door swung shut behind Daniel with an echoing slam. He reached for his pistol and withdrew it but saw no one. Fluorescent light emanated from everywhere and nowhere. Stepping further into the room, Dan grimaced as he saw the darkened walls and fallen debris scattered all over. From somewhere in his memory, he recalled that there had been a bomb planted inside, which had detonated. The rumor at that time was that it had killed his father and Leah. But, in reality, both had escaped unscathed. No one ever learned who planted the device.

Daniel made his way through the debris, keeping his weapon drawn. It was then that the room plunged into almost total darkness. A small fragment of light shone through a crack in the window on the other side of the room. "Welcome to your death, Dan!" a shrill voice rang out. "I knew you would understand my message!" Sara's voice echoed through the warehouse, but Dan couldn't figure out from which direction it came.

Daniel sucked in a breath. "What the hell is going on, sis? Why are you doing all this? What did I do to you?"

"Don't play with me, boy! You know what you've done! You could have stopped Leah from kidnapping us all those years ago. And Jack could have fought to keep us! But he allowed that witch to take us away like nothing mattered—like I never mattered to him!" Sara's voice reverberated through the empty room.

Daniel struggled to adapt to the sudden darkness. With his free hand, he reached into his belt and pulled out a Maglite. Pushing the button on the back with his palm, the light came on and bathed the area in front of him in bright light. Up in the ceiling's corner, Daniel saw a closed-circuit camera. He knew it was on, and it had two-way communication because, in addition to Sara's voice, he heard a grunt followed by several expletives.

"Resourceful, aren't you?" Sara mocked. Daniel said nothing in reply. "Yes, and I loved that performance of yours the other night. I really didn't believe you and Jack could pull it off!"

Daniel didn't understand what his sister meant. "What are you babbling about, Sara?" he asked, knowing it was best to keep her talking as it would keep her distracted.

"Oh, for God's sake, don't you think I *knew* you didn't kill the bastard?" Sara shook her head. She was becoming more irritated with the conversation as the minutes ticked away. She said, "Enough of this shit. I am tired of the game now. Come find me. Let's get this farce over. Prepare yourself, brother; the fun is only beginning!"

Daniel heard another voice yell out, "Don't do it, son! It's a trap!" *Was that really . . . Jack?* Daniel wondered in disbelief. *Had Jack survived?*

"Now, brother, dear, don't listen to him!" Sara continued. "He is doing what he has always done best; he is lying to you. Come here and join us. If you do, I promise I'll let him live. *You*, however, don't get that luxury. I will take pleasure in killing you like I enjoyed killing that whore Patti and all those other bitches who betrayed me!"

That was all Daniel needed. He made the rest of his way to the door on the other side of the room. As though Sara was expecting his arrival, the door opened at just that moment, and Dan felt a gun pressed to his temple. Dan dropped his gun, stepped the rest of the way inside, and saw his father sitting in a wooden chair in the center of the room. Jack's hands were zip-tied behind him, and his feet were tied to the front legs of the chair. If he tried to stand, he would fall face-first to the decaying floor. His naked chest was shaved clean. Deep red bleeding cuts went downward from his chest to his half-clothed legs.

Sara grinned at her brother. "Should I finish the job, Daniel, or do you want the honors?" At his look of horror, Sara shrugged and walked over to Jack. She reached to touch his head, in an almost loving, tender way. But her hand slowly moved toward his throat. Jack squirmed, frightened by what he saw. In Sara's hand, she was clutching the knife she used on her victims.

Daniel leaped at his sister with horrified indignation, pulling another gun and slamming it into her skull as he rammed his body into hers. She expected the move because, at the exact same moment, she whirled on him, thrusting the dagger at his belly. As she did, she drove her foot upward, kicking him hard. "Try that again, you son of a bitch!" she spat in a rage, panting. Sweat and blood oozed down her face. She bent forward, resting her hands on her knees, breathing hard. Sara glowered at her brother.

Daniel, overwhelmed by the attack, suddenly realized he still had his gun in his hand. With a cry of rage, he aimed and pulled the trigger. *This* time, there were real bullets. *This* time, the intended victim fell hard to the floor with a scream of rage. A thud echoed throughout the room. As Daniel watched his sister dying, he knew she would not recover. *This* time, he wept genuine tears.

"Are you okay, son?" Jack asked, wincing with pain. He was making gasping noises, breathing with difficulty. His words were a whisper, but they screamed in Daniel's mind. Daniel helped his father free himself of the restraints around his wrists and ankles, and Jack arched upward, gasping. An obvious concern for Daniel's well-being took precedence over his own injuries and feelings.

Daniel looked down at the blood pooling on the floor from the wound in his belly from Sara's knife. He was sure he would survive. But a cursory analysis of his father's wounds told Daniel a different outcome was in store for him if they did not get him to a hospital. "I'll live," Daniel quipped, smiling. "What about you?" he inquired, even though he was sure what the conclusion was. Time was running out fast. With a grimace, Daniel examined his father's injuries closer.

"Don't worry about me, son. Save yourself. This is my fate. If I live, I will go back to prison. Trust me; it is a fate much worse than Hell if I do." Jack smiled and coughed, wincing as he did.

Daniel inched closer, helping Jack to a sitting position. "At least, *try*," he pleaded with his father. "I can vouch for you. Remember, the plan to stop Sara was *your* idea all along." Jack had suspected what his offspring was capable of when he discovered blood on her bedsheets as a teenager. That was why he isolated his daughter as often as possible. He knew what she was like. It was for not only her safety but also everybody else's. He had, in fact, tried to stop her.

Jack looked his son straight in the eye. "It's worth a shot," he conceded. He allowed Daniel to help him to his feet, and father and son made their way through the darkened warehouse. Daniel opened the door with one hand, and they stepped outside.

The sun was over the horizon now. Exchanging a glance with his son, Jack raised a skeptical eyebrow at him. His eyes adapted to the unexpected brightness of the approaching dawn. He noticed several police cars and an ambulance with its lights flashing parked in the alley. They had kept their sirens off to avoid alerting Sara to their presence. Leah, who stood in the periphery, approached the two men. Bowing her head, she grimaced but was thankful her daughter-in-law had been the final casualty of the killer instead of these men.

Leah wondered what brought Patricia to the house the night she was murdered. Had Sara lured her there? Did she go to confront her daughter? Did Sara turn on her? No one would know now. She watched as the coroner carried

203

her granddaughter's dead body, now encased in the usual white plastic body bag, out of the warehouse on a gurney. They did not zip the bag all the way, leaving one hand exposed. As the stretcher moved across the asphalt, hitting the occasional crack, the hand jostled. It reminded the trio of the movement from an old marionette. They shuddered involuntarily at the sight.

Leah closed her eyes in silent prayer then faced her son and grandson. "Hello, Dan. Hello, Jack." she acknowledged them directly. There were no words left to say. Nothing they could do would bring Patricia back to life. Patti's secrets would, like all those who had suffered at the hands of Sara Saviano, remain buried. Leah hoped Sara's victims all rested in peace. Snapping out of her reverie, Leah rubbed at her face with a trembling hand. She sobbed but hoped neither man noticed. Together, the three of them walked to the waiting ambulance.

From the Publisher

Thank You from the Publisher

Van Rye Publishing, LLC ("VRP") sincerely thanks you for your interest in and purchase of this book.

VRP hopes you will please consider taking a moment to help other readers like you by leaving a rating or review of this book at your favorite online book retailer. Depending on the retailer, you can do so by flipping past the last page of your e-book (to the rating and review page) or by visiting the book's product page (and locating the button for leaving a rating or review).

Thank you!

Resources from the Publisher

Van Rye Publishing, LLC ("VRP") offers the following resources to readers and to writers.

For *readers* who enjoyed this book or found it useful, please consider receiving updates from VRP about new and discounted books like this one. You can do so by following VRP on Facebook (at www.facebook.com/vanryepub) or Twitter (at www.twitter.com/vanryepub).

For *writers* who enjoyed this book or found it useful, please consider having VRP edit, format, or fully publish your own book manuscript. You can find out more and submit your manuscript at VRP's website (at www.vanryepublishing.com).

Thank you again!

About the Author

CHRISTINE E. POSEMATO has always had an interest in writing, and she excelled in writing throughout her school years. She particularly enjoys writing poetry and any kind of fiction. In addition to her love of writing, Christine enjoys spending time with friends and family and playing the piano. Her home state of Arizona is often reflected in her novels, as is the case in her debut murder mystery, thriller, and crime novel titled *Saviano Secrets: A Mafia Murder Mystery*.